THE
GREAT
RECEIVER

THE GREAT RECEIVER

Elena Yates Eulo

Holiday House / *New York*

Library of Congress Cataloging-in-Publication Data

Eulo, Elena Yates.
The great receiver / by Elena Yates Eulo. — 1st ed.
p. cm.
Summary: Returning to high school in the fall, brainy Joey Eastland,
the football team's waterboy, is determined to reinvent himself
by becoming a star player and a "chick magnet."
ISBN 978-0-8234-1888-6 (hardcover)
[1. Football—Fiction.   2. High schools—Fiction.   3. Schools—Fiction.]   I. Title.
PZ7.E869Gr 2008
[Fic] —dc22
2008009002

For my much-loved nephew, Joey West,
in hopes that he will always be a great receiver
of the best life has to offer

Acknowledgments

Most books are fortunate to have one gifted editor. This book has been privileged to enjoy the exceptional talents of two. Thanks go to Suzanne Nelson for her initial editing and inspiring comments and to Julie Amper, whose devoted and skilled hands guided the book home.

Thanks to Samantha Harper Macy and Helen Bisha DePrima, both such talented writers and good friends and willing to read and advise endlessly.

Special thanks go to Vince Valva for donating so many hours and putting so much expertise into designing the Bulldogs' football games and to my son, Ken Eulo, Jr., for his tips on high school quarterbacking.

Finally, I thank my agent, Alison Picard, for her enthusiasm and help in marketing the book, and extend my gratitude to Mary Cash, Editor-in-Chief, for finding Joey and his friends in the half-dead zone and helping them into the end zone.

1

It's a snowy, blustery night in Canton, Ohio. The wind chill factor brings the temperature to below freezing. Up in the stands, people are hidden inside parkas, their faces and necks shrouded in thick woolen scarves, caps pulled low over their foreheads.

But I don't feel the cold.

For the first time ever, our football team, the Lakewood Bulldogs, has reached the state championship game. Wind howls across the field; snow whirls in the downdraft. We're behind the Columbus Cougars, 20-17.

With ten seconds left on the clock, we have the ball on their four-yard line.

The spectators have gone so still they could all be tackle dummies lined up in the stands. The cheerleaders, shivering inside red jackets, hang on to each other, too nervous to make a squeak.

As for me, I'm in the huddle in Cougar territory, waiting to hear if we're going to kick the tying field goal or go for the win.

On the sidelines, our star kicker, Brady Hanson, is kicking practice balls into a net. Waiting for the coach to send in the play, the only things I hear are the whir of wind and the steady thunk of Brady kicking one football after another.

Thunk. Thunk. Thunk.

Nothing rattles Brady. He's a kicking machine. If the coach calls him in, he'll jog calmly onto the field, line up with pro-like precision, and put the ball dead center through the uprights like he's done all season long.

I hope.

Coach Miller paces up and down the sidelines. Assistant Coach Stanley hops along beside him, his collar up against the wind, his right gloved index finger stabbing excitedly toward Brady. But Coach Miller doesn't look at Brady or at anybody else. The expression on his face is why they called him the "Iron Jaw" back in his college quarterback days. The Iron Jaw is capable of any crazy thing, especially right now when he's figuring whether to go for the tie or whether to trust the Great Receiver to save the day.

The Great Receiver is our greatest weapon. He happens to be me, Joey Eastland.

"He's going for the win," Cameron McKey, our star quarterback, mutters in the huddle. Cam wants to throw the ball as much as Brady wants to kick it.

"Naw, he'll bring in Brady," I say, noticing the coach finally glance toward the practice net.

Coach has gone very still. White steam pours from his mouth.

You could hear my heart pounding in Dayton.

All of a sudden a roar rocks the stadium. The coach is waving his arms, motioning for Brian Freeman, a tight end.

A few words with the coach and a slap on the back later, Brian comes running in with the play. My heart stops beating in one quick thud. Sweat rolls down my face; saliva pools in my mouth guard. My hands are cold, shaky, and slick as petroleum jelly. They couldn't hold onto a tree trunk.

"Okay, we're going for it," Brian says nervously. With a ghostlike face, he gives us the play, blow by blow, as if we haven't drilled it a hundred times in practice and done it in almost every game of the season. The call is a fake run, freezing the linebackers while I go in motion and catch the ball in the left corner of the end zone. Every man will block for all he's worth. My job is just to pluck that tight little spiral out of the air, and then we'll all go celebrate.

Cam grins nervously. "You ready, Joey? Guys?"

"Yeah," we all say, putting our hands together. In one play, our season will end.

We break the huddle and line up. For a split second I glance behind me down the field and see it for what it is— not a battlefield, just a long stretch of short, wind-blown, snowy grass with white lines painted on it.

The referee's whistle blows and the play clock starts.

We're down and set. I start in motion, right to left. Like a hoarse bird squawking, Cam yells: *"Forty-three blue, hut-hut . . . hut!"*

The snap is perfect. Football in hand, Cam drops back and fakes the handoff to draw the rush. I'm supposed to be flying into the end zone, but my feet are dead weights. The crowd moans as I trip over my own cleats and stop in my tracks.

3

Looking back over my shoulder, I feel panic set in. It's a blitz! The front line collapses; the defensive linemen are all over Cam.

It's a broken play.

Cam runs left, then breaks right. Through falling snow, I hear the painful *umphs* of bodies colliding.

Cam's scrambling for his life.

Still frozen, I catch a glimpse of Coach Miller. He's looking at me, pounding one hand with the other and yelling, "*Go-Joey-go!*"

The crowd screams along with him. "*Go-Joey-go!*"

Suddenly I'm off, streaking toward the left corner of the end zone, knowing that Cam's looking for me. Through thickening snow, I see him on the run, twisting and squirming. Defensive linemen are charging him from both sides. Any second now, they'll have him.

"*Go-Joey-goooooo!*"

But defensive backs and linebackers are all over me. With the play broken, I have to improvise a way to give Cam a target as he breaks a tackle and heads toward the right sideline.

Racing left to right along the back of the end zone, I'm surrounded by the enemy, but Cam sees me. His arm goes back.

The coach yells, "*Throw the ball!*"

The crowd is one solid scream. "*Throw it! Throw it! Throw it!*"

My heart freezes as Cam starts to go down. Then somehow, at the last minute, he gets the ball off.

From the booth, the announcer's voice screeches. *"Too high! Eastland can't get there! It's over his head!"* With cold sweat streaming into my eyes, I lunge backward in the end zone, stretching to grow taller. Jumping, straining, reaching up. . . . up . . . up into all that blinding white.

From all directions, the other team swarms at me. Sweat races down my face as I look everywhere for the ball.

Amid the swirling white, something comes hurtling down. In a burst of adrenaline I leap toward the brown, spiraling ball as a dozen other hands reach for it, too.

Everybody in the stadium is standing. Feet pound against the stands' metal floor. Voices scream. *"Jo-ey! Jo-ey! Jo-ey!"*

My fingertips graze against pigskin, my fingers growing by inches, gathering it in.

I grit my teeth and hold on, hit from both sides by a diving safety and a charging linebacker. Others pile on top. I end up in a tangled mass of bodies, elbows flying at me, fists jabbing at the ball, trying to force a fumble. But I hang tight. Above the heap, I catch a glimpse of the referee. Both his arms shoot straight up.

Touchdown!

The announcer hollers from the booth. *"What a catch! Incredible catch! Touchdown! Touchdown! Bulldogs win! Bulldogs win!"*

The entire team races toward me as I crawl out from the pile of Cougars. Cam pulls me up. Arms pound my back.

Then they lift me over their heads and carry me across the field.

Cam yells in my ear, "Hey, Joey! You're the best dang receiver in the *whole world,* man! You're the best! You hear me? *You're the best!*"

The crowd goes nuts. The cheerleaders rush at me, calling my name. Coach Miller hollers my name, too. In fact, everyone in the whole stadium is chanting.

"Jo-ey! Jo-ey! Jo-ey!"

"Hey goon-head! Pea-brain! HEY! You listening or sleeping out there?"

"Huh?" Through the fuzz in my head, I looked up to see my older brother Logan glaring at me as he flung an open box through the storage room of our dad's hardware store. Automatically I caught it and started unloading paint rollers. All the metal seats dissolved, along with Coach Miller and Coach Stanley. The other football players were gone, too. Instead of a jersey and football pants, I was wearing a sweatshirt and jeans, and it was no longer a cold December night. It was a Saturday afternoon in late August. Dad had asked Logan and me to unload a new shipment, tag it, and restock the shelves.

"What a space cadet!" my brother said sourly. He was covered in packing debris and dripping sweat. Cowlicks stood up all over his head as if his hair had been glue-sticked here and there. "Let me guess," he sighed, swinging half a dozen stacked utility buckets at me, like he'd like to bop me up side of the head with them. "You were the hero again, right?"

He let go of the buckets and they flew toward me. I caught the lot.

"Touchdown!" he smirked. "Way to go."

I took the buckets, lined them up on the shelf, and then caught several dozen packets of nuts and bolts, followed by a slew of duct tape, mixing sticks, work gloves, and hoses of all sizes. Logan got wicked on the hand-off until he was soon hammering them in all directions.

Catching them, sometimes two or three at a time, brought me back to Earth. I wasn't the Great Receiver. I wasn't any kind of a football player at all. After flubbing my tryout for the second year in a row, I was what the coach called a "hydration therapist."

In other words, I was a frigging water boy.

I had sort of hoped to be called "team assistant," since I not only handed out water bottles, filled the Gatorade tank, and distributed towels, but also put away equipment and helped the team trainer, Karen Harris, load and unload her supplies. I had even learned how to bandage sprains and apply ice to injuries, which I thought might have qualified me to be called "assistant trainer."

Though as Logan put it, I was more the Team Goon, the way I kept dropping things. I even iced Brady Hanson's wrist instead of his ankle. Last night in our first game of the season, I ran onto the field during a time-out with half a dozen water bottles and smashed into Ambrose Morse, a big offensive tackle. Water flew and Ambrose tripped over me. He claimed he'd sprained his ankle until he realized a hurt ankle would take him out of action and dropped the whole charade. Everyone howled as I crawled around picking up bottles.

Logan was right. I wasn't anywhere near Great Receiver material. I wasn't much good off the field either. For starters, I couldn't figure out anything to say to a girl—if one had even wanted to talk to me, which didn't happen much. I didn't have any slick moves. When you came right down to it, the only thing I had going for me was a brain that people called "A-one." If I could have traded my brain for a position on the team, it would have already been in a glass jar in the science lab.

"Comin' atcha!" my brother yelled.

I looked up to see two plastic trash can lids flying at me. I grabbed one under each arm and jogged down the aisle like I was running for a down.

"Too bad they didn't throw paint rollers or garbage can lids during tryouts," Logan said. "You'd have been a sensation."

2

I came down to breakfast on the first day of school to find Mary Pat, Logan's girlfriend, pouring a tiny bit of milk over about three tablespoons of cereal in my brother's bowl.

"Good morning!" she greeted me brightly, drinking half of Logan's orange juice. "There, honey, that's the exact right amount. You'll be shedding that weight in no time."

Logan had come down several pegs from Saturday at the store. He looked gloomily from his bowl to the plate in front of Mary Pat, which was piled with scrambled eggs and toast.

"Hurry up and eat, Logan, or we'll be late." She paused to nibble at her eggs. "Mmm. Very nice." Her eagle eye moved to me. "Why so late this morning, Joey?"

"He couldn't find underwear to match the pattern in his socks," Logan growled, wolfing down the three table-spoons of Raisin Bran in front of him. "I'm still hungry."

Mary Pat waved a scolding finger. "Speak nicely to your brother, honey. It's your belly that's supposed to growl, not your voice."

I looked at Logan, rather interested to see if he'd stand up to her for once, but as usual he just turned red and said nothing.

"Did poor Joey have trouble matching his underwear?" Mary Pat purred, smiling at me over another forkful of eggs. "I always hate that." She ignored Logan choking on the dregs of his milk. "The trick is in the sorting. You put your whites in with your whites and your patterns in with your patterns."

Thinking back to the mess on my bed, half of my closet jumbled into a tangled heap, I nodded. "Yeah, I'll never make that mistake again." It wasn't a good morning. The first day of school, and my clothes sucked and Logan wasn't the only one with cowlicks. There was also a red zit on my nose that I hoped no one would notice.

A cold nose dug under my trouser leg and bumped against my shin. That would be Astro, our setter mix, one of eight pets that included Sarah and Sidney (two garter snakes), Sugar Plum, Angel, Georgia, and Sparky (our four cats), and our other dog, Echo, a rescued pug.

Our animals did *not* include Max, a two-year-old English bulldog, tan with freckles on his nose, standing about twelve inches at the shoulders with bowed legs, barrel chest, and a pump-handle tail. But he was my dog—at least in my mind. Max had been dumped, abused and scared, at the Humane Society where I volunteered. The only one who'd been able to make him stop trembling was me. He'd just cuddled up in my arms and stopped shaking. But there was no room for him in our house, aside from occasional visits, so I had to keep walking out after each of my shifts and leaving him at the shelter, watching me with those soulful eyes of his.

I pinched some egg from my plate and shoved it into Astro's eager mouth just as Echo scampered under the table, demanding her share.

"That's enough, the two of you!" I said sternly, offering Echo a nibble of egg. "Not another bite. If you had it your way, I wouldn't eat at all." They nudged closer, whimpering in excitement, tails wagging violently. Thinking of Max, I gave them each a little more and looked up to find Mary Pat staring at me.

"Your poor nose," she said, distressed. "That pimple could stop traffic."

She whisked her cosmetic kit from the bag hanging from her chair back, rummaged for a white concealer stick, wiped the tip with her napkin, and beckoned me closer.

"Ah . . . it's not so bad," I mumbled, trying to pull away.

"*Not bad*? You could balance a tomato on your nose and it would look better than that thing. Come here." She went to work painting The Pimple That Ate Pompeii and finally nodded. "There. Much better. Now it only looks like you're wearing a little makeup. I should blot it just a tad."

She held up a finger over my juice glass as though ready to dunk it, and I hastily drained the glass.

"You could have saved me a few drops. I need a little liquid, unless you don't mind me spitting on my finger."

"I'd just as soon you used water." I stuck a couple of bits of toast under the table and saw Logan hungrily eyeing them, but the dogs beat him out.

"All right, silly thing," Mary Pat tittered, heading

around the counter that separated the table from the cooking area and sink.

"Logan?" I hissed as the water started running.

"Yeah?"

"Does she pick your nose for you, too?" I asked, grinning. "Well, she does everything else, doesn't she? Chooses your clothes, doesn't she? Or do you like wearing socks with Piglet on them? And I guess you like all those mushy love movies she drags you to? And double-dating with her eighth-grade brother and his seventh-grade girlfriend? Is that fun?"

"Shut up," he snapped, "or I'll—"

"Throw a raisin at me? Oh, I forgot, she took all but three out and they're gone."

"Here we go," Mary Pat cooed, coming back with a damp finger held carefully over a dishrag. She leaned over me like a museum restorer repairing a Michelangelo. Finally she drew back to examine the results. "That's nice. Now you only look a tiny bit red and a tiny bit made up. Your nose could almost pass for normal."

Mom came in lugging my three-year-old squirming brother Scott under one arm. Her purse swung from one shoulder, and Scott's old diaper bag weighted down the other, with its load of stuffed animals, food, toys, and a raggedy blanket that he insisted on sleeping with. He'll probably still be using it when he's thirty.

"Good morning, everybody!" Mom said brightly, trying not to trip on Sugar Plum, her favorite cat, who was purring eagerly and weaving in and out between her feet.

"Hi, Mom!" Logan and I chorused on top of Mary Pat's happy "Good morning, Mrs. Eastland!"

"Hurry, Joey," Mom said, frowning at my full plate. "We should have been out of here five minutes ago! Oh, you're eating Logan's eggs, Mary Pat? He wasn't hungry?"

"He has love handles," Mary Pat explained cheerfully.

"And we know we can't have those ugly things," I said spitefully, following Mom out of the kitchen as my brother scowled back.

"Are you driving Logan to school, Mary Pat?" she called from the front door. She'd managed to wrestle it open without dropping her purse, the diaper bag, or my little brother.

"Yes, ma'am!" Mary Pat called back. "I'll be driving him every day from now on, not to worry."

"All right. Drive carefully. Joey, out of here! What are you doing?"

"Uh . . ." I had stopped to look at the clownishly red-and-white nose reflecting back at me in the hall mirror.

"Get marching!" Mom suddenly caught sight of an open tank in the living room. "Oh, no! P.S. left the lid off the tank again." My little brother was nicknamed P.S. because they hadn't expected to have any more kids after me until he surprised them. "Get Sugar Plum quick!" she added. As I scooped up our white cat, Mom stuck her head back in the door and bellowed: "Logan! The tank is open and Sarah and Sidney are out! Get them back in the tank before you leave for school, or the cats will be after them. I think they're in the sofa again."

Logan appeared in the kitchen door and trudged toward the couch, followed by Mary Pat, who shrank back nervously as he started to look behind the pillows.

"I'm not that crazy about snakes," she murmured, sounding timid for her. "I'd rather those baby squirrels you were nursing, or the baby porcupine."

"I had to take those to the wildlife release lady, along with the litter of skunks. Garter snakes won't hurt you . . . oh, good, there's one of them," Mom added.

Mary Pat screeched and backed up as Logan's hand emerged from inside the couch with what appeared to be Sidney wriggling between his fingers.

"P.S. just won't leave the tank alone," Mom said. "Put Sidney back in the tank, Logan. Sarah will be in the sofa somewhere, thank you, dear. We're off. Joey, you can set Sugar Plum down. Logan will manage now."

As she closed the door, I heard Mary Pat scream, *"Don't get that thing close to me!"*

Mom's old minivan sat beside Mary Pat's new sports car in the driveway.

"Mom . . . do you think Mary Pat will pick out Logan's underwear when they're married?"

"He wears underwear?" Mom asked absently.

"*Huh?* You mean he doesn't . . . ?"

"I mean I haven't had time to do the laundry in almost two weeks. If he's found clean underwear, it's more than I have. Stop wiggling, P.S. Any more squirms and I swear you'll hit the dust. I'm about to wilt in this heat. You hot, Joey?"

"I'm fine," I lied. It was one of those late August days

when the air feels so heavy you can't fight your way through it, but a good athlete functions in any kind of weather.

Mom let her bags drop to the ground and popped my little brother into his car seat in the back. "Okay, we're off."

"Want to sit with Joey, want to sit with Joey," P.S. chanted.

"Joey, do you mind?"

I got out of the front and plopped down beside my brother in the back. Immediately he started throwing dry Cheerios at me and laughing his butt off.

If I was ever as happy as P.S., I can't remember when. But Dad says my only trouble is a bad attack of male hormones setting in now that I'm almost fifteen. I asked him if hormones made you nuts, and he said, "Whew." Then I asked him if they make you feel like a second-class citizen. "Like a reject of Mars," he said.

We headed toward the high school, me almost wishing that Mary Pat had offered me a ride, too. Anything was better than being dropped off by your mom. I made an immediate decision to ride my bike tomorrow.

"Got your eye on a cute girl yet?" Mom asked over her shoulder.

Cringing, I said, "Nope." Actually I'd had my eye on half a dozen since last year. But none seemed to have an eye on me. And I didn't think I'd be interested in any girl who would accept a date with me. Maybe I'd start dating next year when I was a junior. Or when I was a senior. Or when I was forty. Or even older. Maybe I could advertise: Sixty-year-old man seeking first kiss.

I studied pictures of guys in magazines to see what I should look like, and watched how studs acted in movies, trying to copy their moves. I kept my eye on Cam McKey at school, but I couldn't pick up any of his tricks. Bitterly I wondered why I had to be born with brains instead of cool, and why I had to be so good at catching paintbrushes and lacquer cans instead of footballs.

"Hmm," Mom said.

I waited for the inevitable.

"I was thinking you'd ask that friend of yours out. Samantha, the one who helps out at the Society. She's very cute and smart and loves animals."

"Sam and I are just friends." Mom had only suggested this at least half a dozen times and been told the same thing over and over.

"*Best* friends, right?"

"Yeah. And best friends don't date." They also didn't kiss, but I didn't add that bit of info.

"Sometimes best friends make the best dates. Your dad and I were best friends before we dated," she said fondly.

"Yeah, and look where it landed you. Just kidding," I added quickly.

She pulled into the school parking lot and inched along behind about ten other cars. "Have a good day, okay? Remember, think positive. You're terrific."

"Mom . . . please."

"I mean it."

"Okay, thanks," I mumbled, feeling anything but terrific. But then Mom had been irrationally crazy about me since I was born, even going so far as to think I was good-looking. She pulled to the curb and waited for me to get out, then turned around to give me a concerned look when I just sat there, drooped beside P.S.

"What's wrong, Joey? Are you getting sick? I think this football team stuff is zapping you."

"Yeah, carrying water bottles and towels is exhausting. I don't know how I stand up under it."

"Honey, I know you wanted to make the team, but frankly, I'm just as glad it turned out this way. Football is such a dangerous sport. I'd be worrying every minute if you were out there playing. I hear they have *ambulances* outside the field."

"One ambulance," I said wearily. "And the only one who was in it last season was a little boy from the top of the stands who got a nosebleed."

She looked at me unhappily, caught between sympathy for me and relief that I was safely off the field of play. I stopped dropping Cheerios in P.S.'s plastic bag and looked back at her. She was wearing jeans and the oversized sweatshirt she wore to work at the Humane Society. It had a dog on it with the logo: *Have you hugged your pet today?* Her brown hair was short and straight and she hardly ever wore makeup. She was always trying to lose fifteen pounds. It got harder to lose weight, she claimed, after forty. Still there was something about her that was easy to look at. When you were with her, you knew you counted.

"There are jocks," she murmured tenderly, "and there are thinkers. You . . ."

"Yeah, yeah, I know. I'm a jerky nerdy thinker."

"Being a thinker is good; you'll find that out someday."

She reached back to pat my leg. "Get a move on, kiddo. P.S. is due at Grandma's and then I'm off to the dogs. So to speak."

I opened the car door and looked around to see if anybody in the crowd streaming toward the high school front steps was a friend. The truth was that I didn't have many. We had been in Lakewood over a year, since Dad sold his old hardware store and bought a bigger one here. I still felt out of the loop, which was mainly composed of the richest, most athletic, and best-looking kids—the ones with that indefinable cool. There was no way I would ever fit into that group. They barely knew I existed.

Nancy Frazier, queen of the loop, flew past our car with her long brown ponytail flipping up and down as she ran. She was something to see, but the only one *she* had eyes for was Cam McKey.

My stomach felt like I'd eaten nails for breakfast.

"Joey?" Mom murmured.

"Okay, I'm outta here."

"Bye-bye, Joey," P.S. said sadly.

I summoned a smile and opened my car door. "Bye, big guy. Later."

Just take a deep breath and imagine you're the Great Receiver, I told myself, stepping from the car. *Do everything the way he'd do it if he were just getting to school. Stay laid-back and cool. Don't try to make eye contact. When you're popular, other people try to make eye contact with you, not the other way round. Walk tall. Nothin' to it.*

It was a brand-new school year, a whole new chance to reinvent myself. Somehow I had to pull it off.

3

The only thing I could think about was the red zit on my nose. The Great Receiver never had a zit in his life.

Trying to catch a glimpse of my face in the car window, I stepped backward and tripped over the curb. Naturally, Ashley Parker, Nancy Frazier's best friend, was just passing by. Ashley had curly blond hair and eyelashes longer than a granddaddy longlegs. As usual she looked mysterious and glamorous.

Of course she had to say it.

"Have a good trip?" Her mysterious look melted and she laughed.

"Yeah," I mumbled. "Better than going to Chicago."

She giggled again as I stumbled toward the front steps at the school entrance.

How come every time I tried to be the Great Receiver, I ended up being a clown? A few other kids had caught what happened, and they were laughing, too. Like they'd laughed at tryouts when I dropped every ball and fell over the hurdles. My running had real style, too— pigeon-toed, with my kneecaps banging together.

Why couldn't I have run like I do at night by myself,

streaking down the street so fast you'd think I was running down a dark alley with a TV set under each arm? Why couldn't I catch balls like I do when Dad throws them to me in the park? But nooo . . . there had to be a curse on me that made me screw up every single time I tried to do something that really mattered.

"You're good, Joey," Dad said when the list came out and I wasn't on it. "Don't let an hour-long tryout tell you any different."

I felt bad for his sake, too. Somehow he found time in his packed schedule to go to the park with me, time to throw footballs to me and clock my running on the track. I think he'd secretly wanted me to make the team as much as I'd wanted to make it.

"Yeah." I nodded. "Sure. Not a problem." It was the worst night of my life. Imagine not even being good enough to be on the worst team in the district, a team looking for new players. But you don't make a team looking to rebuild if you miss every ball, fall on the hurdles, and have to pull up on the track with a stitch in your side, unable to catch your breath.

Nerves. All nerves.

I was so wrapped up in my misery that at first I didn't hear the voice calling me.

"Hey, *Joey*! Can you *hear* already?" Samantha Burton's long brown hair flew in every direction as she jogged up the steps behind me.

"Hey," I said with a weak grin.

"I've been yelling my head off at you," she said, her

dark eyes snapping at me from behind her glasses. "What's your problem?"

"I just fell on my butt in front of Ashley Parker."

"That snob?" Sam sniffed. "Why should you care what she thinks?"

"Well . . ." I hesitated. Sam wouldn't care about my interest in another girl, whatever Mom's sly hopes. We were best friends, nothing more. Still . . .

Sam snorted. "Forget her. If a deep thought ever accidentally fell into that one's head, she'd start screaming from fear."

"She and Nancy are in Honors Reading and Language Arts," I reminded her. Besides, Ice Maiden Ashley knew things. Important and deep things.

Sam shrugged and changed the subject. "Did Perry Toomey call you over the weekend about Mrs. Cunningham's 'Power of Understanding' project?"

"He called." Perry had volunteered to be Mrs. Cunningham's student aide on Lakewood High's participation in a project that would stretch across the world, with teens learning and writing about other cultures. Several of the top essays would be read at the United Nations and translated into many languages.

"Nice of Perry to volunteer to help," Sam said approvingly.

"That bootlicker? He would have offered to do her laundry and clean out her freezer if she'd just given him a hint."

Sam smiled, looking close to pretty with all that eagerness

in her eyes. "With the mess the world is in today, this will really be important. Our only solution to world peace is understanding and tolerance, right?"

I nodded uneasily. "He said you and I would be in his group. Let me rephrase that. He said we'd be under his leadership, along with Kelsey Magnum and Ted Wyatt, who'll be doing the artwork."

"They're both wonderful!" she said excitedly. "Ted did the park mural; did you see it? And most of the animation for last year's city environmental campaign! And Kelsey's watercolors—"

"I told Perry to take my name off his list. I can't do it."

Her head whipped around like she was a rattlesnake and I had just stepped on her tail. "What?"

"It's starting too early, Sam. We haven't even had a class, and Mrs. C. is already charging at us."

"She's only the best teacher in the entire school!" Sam snapped. "Besides it's good to start early before we're bogged down in homework and tests."

"It won't work out."

"Please don't tell me that you're turning down the most important project we've ever had a chance to participate in!"

"Uh, yeah." I didn't like the look on her face.

"You're kidding, right? Mrs. C. is depending on her top students for this. Your essays are always the best. This is the world we're talking about, Joey. I mean, wow, this project is about trying to put the *world* together through mutual understanding! You do get what I'm saying, right?"

"Sam, I have football."

"FOOTBALL?" she shrieked, losing it. "YOU MEAN

THAT STUPID CARTING-WATER-AROUND FLUNKY THING YOU DO?"

We had just walked inside the main doors to the building. There wasn't one kid in the lobby whose head wasn't turned our way, and every face had a big fat smirk on it.

"Thanks a lot," I mumbled, looking for a loose floorboard to crawl under.

Her face wilted. "I'm sorry, Joey," she whispered.

I wondered why she'd screamed out the humiliating stuff and whispered the apology. But who cared? It was what everyone was thinking anyhow.

"You're not really a flunky," she added. "Even if you do let them treat you like one."

"You're a born diplomat, Sam. You ought to get a job as an ambassador after you graduate from college."

She looked at me sideways. "About 'The Power of Understanding' . . ."

"Forget it."

Her mouth grew fangs. "You make me so mad I could spit!" She stomped her foot. On top of my big toe. I dropped my notebook and papers flew.

"Great, Sam, just really terrific," I mumbled.

She sighed and helped me pick everything up, and we found ourselves kneeling an inch apart and looking right into each other's faces.

For a few seconds we just stared, and then she whispered: "Ah, Joey?"

"Yeah?"

"Is that dust or . . . or powder on your nose?" We both scrambled to our feet.

Of course Cam McKey *would* be passing by exactly at that moment, and he had ears like an elephant's. He had been known to pick up a play from the other team's sidelines in the middle of a crowd cheer.

"EASTLAND'S WEARING POWDER!" he announced to the hall at large. "AND A BLOB OF RED LIPSTICK ON HIS NOSE!" He leaned in for a closer look, shuddered, and jumped back. "Oops, sorry, it's just a zit. I thought from the size of it . . . Seriously, red looks great on you, dude. You've found your color."

His friend, Matt Burris, was honking through his nose. It was a real circus. What Cam and his group had against me, I couldn't say, other than they were good at scenting out weakness and insecurity.

"I'm getting out of here," Sam said loftily. "I have no time for such nonsense. I'd advise you to follow me." She turned on her heel and took off toward the stairs, head held high and gaining yardage by the second. When she hit the stairs, she took them two at a time.

I wondered if Sam had ever thought of going out for track and field.

"Hey, Eastland," Cam yelled across the lobby. "Keep your nose away from my water bottle this afternoon. I won't know if I'm drinking water or if it's your zit gushing."

While Cam ran around yelling "Fire!" and fanning his nose, his buddies roaring with laughter, I crammed papers back into my notebook and stumbled up the stairs.

Perry Toomey appeared out of nowhere, shaking his head pityingly as he churned up the steps beside me. "I see you let the creeps make an idiot out of you, Joey." Mr. Know-It-All was in the Debate Club, the Chess Club, the Latin Club, the Beta Club, the Science Club, and Students for the Preservation of Endangered Species. He also played first seat clarinet for the marching band and got all A's.

"Just remind yourself," he said, "that relatively speaking, you're a lot smarter than that bunch." He jerked his pointy little chin toward Cam and his buds. With a chin like his, he could be a prosecutor and never have to point a finger.

"Relatively speaking?" I repeated.

"Meaning that if you put their brains together, you'd be lucky to come up with a thimbleful of gray stuff."

"And I have a thimbleful?"

He shrugged. "More or less."

"Jeez, Perry, you've made my day. Uh . . . about the international project. I'm sorry I can't do it but . . ."

"We'll see."

"See what? I already told you. I can't do it."

"That may or may not be," he said in a maddeningly superior tone. "Busy people can always find time. Look at me. I'm even in the process of inventing a solar helicopter."

"Perry, I am not going to do the project, end of subject," I said hastily, not wanting to get him started on the helicopter he'd been working on for more than two years.

"I admire your resistance. I really do. Well, see you in biology. By the way, I was thinking of taking you on as a lab partner. The class is of such poor quality that you're the best available." He blew out a sigh. "Being brilliant is not always easy. Sometimes it's a burden and a struggle to be

25

surrounded by such mediocrity. However, not to worry. I should be able to pull you through adequately." He started to move toward his own homeroom.

"Wait! I don't think I—"

"I'll tell Mr. Adams. Later."

Tommy Brink, one of Cam's friends from the football team, passed me, snickering. "Headline in Dork Gazette: 'Tombstone and Red Nose Join Forces in Curve-busting.' Maybe Tombstone can boil you up some zit cream in one of his test tubes."

He galloped down the hall ahead of Perry, leaving me to my misery. Most days it took at least an hour or two to make a complete idiot of myself. Today I had outdone myself.

4

Things went from bad to worse. Just before sophomore Honors Reading and Language Arts started, Nancy Frazier, who sat across from me and in front of Ashley Parker, was telling Ashley about a party she'd gone to where the ratio of guys to girls was five to one. "I kid you not, I walked in to find myself on a total dude ranch." A pirate ship or dude ranch meant there were mainly guys. A chick farm meant mainly girls.

"Cam and Matt were on their white-water rafting trip," Nancy said. "You were grounded, as usual. I didn't think there would be any harm in going alone. I mean it was a *party*."

"You mean Tommy Brink's party, right?" Ashley murmured.

"Yes, and his parents were out for the night."

"Hmm." Several diamond-bright teeth bit into her lower lip as she got deeper into the idea. "Sounds verrry interesting."

"It was amazing. Guys lined up, drooling. I told Tommy right away that I was out of there. Cam would have gone nuts if he'd heard I'd stayed. And if my mom ever found me in a house with that kind of ratio and no adults, I'd be in lockdown for a month."

A mischievous look stole across Ashley's face. "I wish I'd been there. I love that kind of ratio."

"That's why you *live* in lockdown, girl."

Something came over me. Like stupidity. I leaned across the aisle like I was in the loop and said, "I'd risk lockdown to party on a chick farm." I grimaced at my own words, but it was too late to stuff them back in my mouth.

The way Nancy turned and stared at me, I thought my zit must have grown bigger than my nose by now.

"Pardon me?" she snapped.

"I . . . I was saying I'd like to be on the . . . the chick farm . . ."

"Oh, yes?" she said icily. "And just what would you do if you were there? On the chick farm, I mean."

"Well . . ." I felt my neck heating up. The heat shot up into my face. "Uh . . . just . . . just talk, I guess."

By now kids all around us were wheezing, trying not to laugh.

"Talk," Nancy repeated. "It would hardly be worth the trip then, would it?" She flipped her ponytail at me and turned away.

Ashley looked at me playfully and winked, then leaned up to whisper in Nancy's ear. Whatever she said made Nancy laugh uncontrollably.

I slid further down in my seat, wishing I were invisible. (But she *did* wink at me, part of me whispered.)

Just then Mrs. Cunningham came into the room. I

didn't pay much attention until it became clear that a laser beam was boring through my head. When I looked up, Mrs. C. was glaring at me. I hunched over my desk and started rummaging through my notebook.

"*Joey Eastland!*" she announced. "I will see you after class, please. My desk."

I kept my eyes down, thumbing through papers and trying not to look her in the eye. It was impossible. She waited until I finally looked up. I wished I hadn't. Mrs. C. had bulletlike eyes, black and piercing. You couldn't budge her with a bulldozer.

"May I have some sign of acknowledgment, Eastland?" she asked, tapping a pen against the corner of her desk. "Some small token of recognition that I am in the room and speaking to you?"

"Yes ma'am," I said miserably.

"I presume I'll have the pleasure of your company after class, as requested?"

I nodded, and Nancy giggled.

I straightened in my seat and gritted my teeth, ready for battle. One thing for sure, people were going to stop ordering me around. If I said I was turning down "The Power of Understanding," I was turning it down, and that was that. I would use the University of Tennessee's famous coach Bowden Wyatt's advice to defensive players: Take the shortest route to the ball and arrive in a bad humor.

"Class," Mrs. C. said briskly, "I presume you've all completed your summer reading. Let's begin with a discussion on *I Know Why the Caged Bird Sings.*"

29

I got out my notes, thinking of all the heroic people who had emerged from terrible adversity with their souls intact. I hoped I had that courage. Mrs. C. was a powerful woman, but she was not going to cage me, and I was not going to sing.

5

"No. Way. Jo. Sé." Mrs. C. accented every syllable. She didn't look at all impressed that I had marched right up to her desk and firmly refused to participate in the international peace project.

"I'm sorry, but I'm involved with football this semester," I explained, ignoring the acidy panic that flooded my stomach. "I won't have time for the project. It's extracurricular, isn't it?"

"Not for you, it isn't. You're one of the top students in my honors class, and I expect it of you."

I faced her down, remembering that Shug Jordan, Auburn's winningest football coach, had spurred on his team against a formidable opponent by reminding them that Goliath had been a forty-point favorite over David.

"It's not only writing the paper," I said, trying not to flinch under her stony gaze, "there'll also be a lot of research. And rewriting. And won't you be meeting after school?"

"We will. Twice a week. I will be rotating meetings with two teams. That makes ten outstanding students in our school who will be helping in this important international plan to unite the world through the investigation of different cultures and sharing ideas by its youthful scholars—including you, Eastland. You're in the most select group, I might add. I have given you the best artists in the school, because I think your team might have a real chance to produce an exceptional project."

"I'm sorry, but I have to say no," I said, quaking in my sneakers.

She wagged her head from side to side, faster than somebody watching a tennis match. "You're not getting out of this. Not a chance, baby. No way, uh-uh."

"But—" By this time Goliath was an eighty-point favorite over David.

"Don't give me any lip, Eastland. I put a lot of work into you, including all those extra sessions last year, helping you with that paper on animal cruelty. It got your mother's Humane Society five thousand dollars, I seem to remember."

I nodded weakly. It was true.

"I expect payback now."

"But . . . but . . ."

"You *will* pay me back, you hear me? *No*-body takes the blood and guts out of Maureen Cunningham without delivering the goods in return. *You are going to write an essay for 'The Power of Understanding.' Do I make myself clear?*" She set her jaw.

"I've got an obligation to the football team," I said hoarsely, feeling myself about to cave. "I promised the coach." If I gave in now, she would own me.

"The coach will get used to living with one less hydration therapist, Eastland."

"Not the coach. It . . . eh . . . it's Karen Harris, the team trainer. She's a physical therapist, you know, which is a field that has always kind of interested me."

She turned her X-ray eyes on me. "It has, huh? I thought you were headed toward arguing the law."

"Me? I don't argue much about anything."

Mrs. C. didn't bat an eyelash.

"Instead of being a lawyer, who knows, I might . . . um . . . someday be a physical therapist," I blundered on, improvising. Clearly I needed something to swing the balance.

Her eyes dug into me like grappling hooks.

"There's something about your interest in this team that you're not telling me," she said finally. "You got a thing about sports, Joey? Is that it? Do you wish you were playing on this team?"

There was understanding in her face now. She waited for my answer, but my Adam's apple was doing a lasso act with my tonsils. Finally I shook my head.

"No ma'am," I managed to say. "Nothing like that."

"I'm wrong, huh?" She just about smiled. "I don't think so, but we'll let it go, okay? I've been around a lot of people who wanted what they couldn't have, and I know that feeling like I know my own heartbeat. Tell you what. I'll work around Coach Miller's schedule. But one thing, Eastland."

"What's that?" I couldn't help smiling at her some, but I still had a raw feeling inside.

33

"When football season is over, you belong to me," she said. "No ifs, ands, or buts. Deal?"

I took the powerful hand she held out, all long, red curved nails and strong fingers. It felt like a talon had grabbed hold of me.

"Deal," I muttered.

Sam was waiting outside the classroom. She stuck a candy bar at me.

"What's that for?" I said, not taking it.

"I thought you'd likely need some comfort food."

"Why?"

"When you're beaten, you always need to pamper yourself. Or the defeat is just too awful."

"If I had a candy bar for every defeat I suffer, Sam, I'd need a wheelbarrow to carry them all."

"So you don't want it?" She started to stick it back in her bag.

I grabbed it, peeled the wrapper off, and took a big bite of chocolate, almonds, and coconut. She was right. I immediately felt a little better.

"How come you were so sure she would win?" I asked, taking another bite.

"It's like pitting a gerbil against a crocodile," she explained.

"Lovely of you to put it that way."

"Don't look like that," she said kindly. "You really are amazing, persevering against the horrible odds you put yourself up against all the time. You just never know when to quit. I admire that a lot—that you won't quit." She looked at me affectionately. "Believe it or not, that very thing is going to make you a big winner someday."

I didn't understand exactly what she was saying, but it didn't sound much like an insult. All in all, it was the best I'd felt all day. Then a familiar laugh ruined it all. Nancy Frazier stood on her tiptoes, whispering something into Cam McKey's ear between giggles.

Cam looked at her with his mouth hanging open in astonishment, then reached up with a practiced gesture to scrape his blond hair off his forehead.

"Eastland on a chick farm," he said, wagging his head sorrowfully, his arm draped around Nancy's neck. "How pitiful would that be?"

6

With the second game looming, practices became more like endurance contests, subjecting the first man to collapse on the playing field to jeers and taunts from his sweaty, upright comrades. We had won our first game, but it had been an out-of-conference game with a small parochial school not known for its football. The Morrison Tigers would be our first real test this coming Friday and Coach Miller was pushing the team hard.

"As Bear Bryant used to say," Coach droned, quoting his favorite mentor for about the tenth time, "I make my practices real hard, because if a player is a quitter, I want him to quit in practice, not in a game."

While the football players stretched and exercised and then broke off into drills with position coaches, I doled out liquids and towels. I also set up hurdles and stocked ice and bandages for Karen Harris. Then I helped offensive guard, José Lopez, stretch out his legs, and put an ice wrap on linebacker Ricardo Gonzalez's knee. I was even lower than a water boy. Sam was right. I was nothing more than a flunky around the field.

Between chores and my low-down mood, it took a

while for me to notice that every player looked to have gotten smacked by a wet sack.

"What's up?" I asked Brady Hanson. He was on break, slumped down on the bleachers in a pool of his own sweat.

"The principal suspended Matt Burris. He can't play on the team. You believe that rotten luck?" Brady shook his head, totally disgusted.

Matt was a junior like Cam and had been the team's star wide receiver last year. Not only was he fast, but he also had a decent pair of hands and was aggressive in a crunch. When he had to, he could block like a lineman and had been instrumental in last week's win.

I stared at Brady. "Why can't he play? What happened?"

He was moodily watching Cam throw passes to several guys on the team, mostly incomplete. "Tombstone is what happened. He's the one who got Matt in trouble. It all went down this afternoon."

"Perry Toomey?" As obnoxious as Perry could be, he was the last kid in the school I could imagine causing any problems for Matt Burris.

"Tombstone is a nerdy jerk who ought to eat maggots and die," Brady said. He cast an evil eye my way. "You got a problem with that?"

"Who, me?" I said that a lot. "What did he do?"

"Rumor on the street has it that Tombstone ratted on Matt for stealing the geometry lesson plan out of Mr. Tyson's desk. It had every test for the first semester. Tombstone saw him steal it and ran straight to the teacher. Now Matt can't play ball, all because of some little know-it-all rat. What are we supposed to do for a wide receiver? Cam is *not* happy."

That would be putting it mildly, I thought. To a quarterback, the loss of his best receiver is equivalent to losing his right hand. Our second wide receiver, Wayne Yeager, was only okay. He ran like a sloth, but could usually catch the ball unless it was thrown too hard or too far or under too much coverage. Against aggressive high-pressure teams, he sucked, which tended to make Cam look like he sucked, too. If there was anything Cam hated, it was looking bad.

But how could you be a decent quarterback if nobody could catch anything you threw? Except possibly the other team, and that was another problem.

"We still have good defense," I muttered, but I could see Brady wasn't listening anymore.

He heaved himself from the bleachers and went down to practice with the kicking team, leaving me to consider what we had, beyond an excellent defense. We had good running, especially from our star running back, Tony Gilmore, who was only 5'5" in cleats but a speedster at halfback; and our all-star fullback, Melvin Barr, who had been known to drag three tacklers for a five-yard gain. Brian Freeman, known as Mr. Freeze, was a strong tight end, catching almost any short quick pass that was thrown to him; he was also known for keeping his head under pressure. José Lopez was as big and mean as guards come, if you tried to sack our quarterback. Our kicking team was excellent, with our center, George White, laying claim to a pair of steady hands, and Brady kicking over 90 percent of field goals from thirty yards or under. But without the ability to pass the long ball, we would come up short offensively.

By the end of the day, the main contender for wide receiver was Tommy Brink, who was a backup running back. The worst thing about Tommy as wide receiver was that, like Wayne, he had no hands. He kept trying to catch the ball against his chest, and it kept bouncing off his body. I pictured all the cans, buckets, and paint rollers I had caught over the years at Dad's hardware stores and thought what a shame it was that Tommy had never hired on with Dad as a stocker.

Cam kept throwing the ball, and Tommy kept missing it.

Tommy hollered, "Come on, man! Give me a break. The idea is to make it catchable!"

Disgusted, Cam threw up his arms and cursed.

This morning Tommy had been in the thick of Cam's crowd, laughing at me. He wasn't laughing now. Coach Miller wasn't laughing either. It was his first year as coach. He'd taken over a lackluster football program that had all but disappeared under the absentminded ten-year reign of Coach Walker Seymour, who had finally retired. With the mess Seymour had left behind him, Coach Miller had had his hands full on day one. The loss of Matt put him even more under the gun. Still, the Iron Jaw kept his cool, speaking in a low tone to Assistant Coach Stanley, who was also receiver coach.

It was Coach Stanley who was yelling. "You're stopping in midstride out there, Tom—you gotta keep running, and I mean *go*! Cam's throw will lead you into your pass pattern. Got that? You'll have to catch up to the ball. While running your routes, *he will be leading you!*"

"I know that," Tommy said, flicking off beads of sweat.

"Couldn't prove it by what we just saw." Coach Stanley blew his whistle and motioned to Cam. "C'mon back! We're gonna run it again!"

Tommy wiped off more sweat and dug in for another go. He looked like he would have preferred biting off chicken heads to running another play with Cam.

Finally, just after six-thirty, the players and coaches dragged themselves out to the parking lot and piled into cars, knowing their season would be even worse than usual.

For the Bulldogs, who were usually last in our division, that was saying a lot.

I had volunteered to put away the hurdles and lock up the equipment room, but I waited to finish up until the last person had gone. I was alone under the late sun. The warm wind blew harder against my neck.

Our second game would take place on our own field. Homecoming. I could hardly breathe thinking what it must be like to be in uniform, running from the locker room and through the cheerleaders' formation onto the field, with the crowd cheering, pompoms shaking, and streamers flying.

I'd only played football before on two flag teams. I'd been good, too, but that was back in my old hometown. Mom wouldn't allow me to play Pop Warner, no matter how hard I'd begged. I was too young, she'd said, and the Pop Warner League allowed tackling, which was too dangerous. In the three years since I'd played flag, I'd dreamed of making the high school team. But if I hadn't even made JV last year, how was I supposed to make varsity this year, especially since I'd been lousy again?

Something stung at my eyes as I took a long look around to make sure I was really alone before stripping off my shirt. All this belonged to me now.

I warmed up first and then did a few practice laps around the field, stretching out my long legs. When I was running, I wasn't King Flunky. I was a hawk with a golden eye, soaring above all the rest. Cruising around the field looking for prey now—some guard who thought he could beat me to the ball or bring me down. It would never happen. My ears hummed as I put on speed.

By the time I got to the hurdles, I was on fire. Run and jump, run and jump, run and jump. Clean jumping. Nothing fell over. I sailed through the course once, then again. Then a third time, until my eyes were so full of sweat they were burning.

I grinned at the field I'd just conquered. Then I slumped to my knees and put my head in my hands. What a joke. I wasn't on the team. Would never be on the team.

And Matt threw it all away by acting like a jerk.

I don't know how much later it was when I finally got up and started putting away the hurdles. I had to hurry. Mom would worry if I was late for dinner. Never in my life had I felt less hungry.

7

Mom wasn't hungry either. "The vet had to put down fifteen dogs and twenty-two cats today." Her eyes welled up. "*Fifteen dogs . . . twenty-two . . .*" she sobbed. "I wanted to bring every last one of them home with me."

"Um . . ." Dad began worriedly. "We already have the two snakes, and let's see, two dogs and, ah . . . three cats, isn't it?"

A few tears spilled down Mom's cheeks. "Four cats. Remember we kept that little white one with black feet— Sugar Plum—that we raised from a week old? We thought she wouldn't live and grew too attached to her to give her up."

"We did?" Dad feverishly wiped turkey sauce from his lips. "I feel very badly about those poor animals, sweetheart. But—but we have a modest little house, you know. More like a one-animal house, not a seven—make that eight animal house. The animals already have the majority." He laughed nervously. "One more and they might get too cramped and decide to vote us out onto the streets." He looked a little dejected that our house was so small. He also looked whipped from the day's work.

Logan looked miserable, too, haunted by the upcoming SAT exam. He dreamed of going to Xavier College and then veterinary school. But last spring's SAT had been a disaster. Since the awful morning he'd gone on-line to see his score, he had felt as if the sky had fallen.

"1020" he had repeated all spring and summer, as if he were learning a new language. He had never gotten less than a B on his report card. Mostly, he got A's. It was impossible that he had gotten only 1020 out of a possible 2400. It couldn't have happened. But it had. And now he was desperately afraid it would happen again when he retook the test.

To make it even worse, Mary Pat had scored 2230. Logan thought her score could be a school record. Just as he thought his might have broken the record for low score.

"It was horrible at school today," Logan said. "People kept talking about where they were applying to college and bragging about their great SAT scores. Then they'd ask about mine. I'd say 1020. There would be this dead silence and they'd squint at me like they were seeing somebody they'd never met. There I was, surrounded by all the other accelerated students, all with spectacular SAT scores except me. And Mary Pat was there to see it happen," he finished gloomily.

"You just got nervous last time," Dad said. "Your second SAT will come out fine."

"If I got nervous before, I could get nervous again," Logan said despairingly. "Or what if I'm just an idiot? What if all this time I thought I was smart because Mary Pat was cramming my head full of facts before every test?

I'll never get into Xavier or even state if I score another 1020."

"Logan, you're a good student," Mom said. "But things happen. It doesn't hurt to gear down our expectations. We've got a nice little community college right here in Lakewood."

Logan groaned, accidentally putting an elbow into his spaghetti and ground turkey sauce. "What if I flunk out of community college?"

"Yum," P.S. said, shoveling in his cut spaghetti, oblivious to exam scores. Turkey sauce was all over his face. He didn't know there were other kinds of meat sauce.

Mom hadn't made vegetarians of us yet, but red meat never came to our table. If we weren't eating veggie burgers, it was turkey fajitas or soy sausage.

"If you flunk out of community college," Mom said calmly, making Logan blanch, "then you can always go to a trade school or become a veterinary assistant. That way, even though you wouldn't be a veterinarian, you'd be working with one." Mom's pessimism dated back to her own high school days when she wanted to be a drum majorette. "I twirled that baton until my fingers were blistered," she often told us. "It got to where it was almost part of my hand. Dropping my own fingers was as likely as dropping that baton."

Except, of course, she had dropped it. Not once, but three times during the tryouts. Needless to say she hadn't made majorette. The horrible lesson she had learned that day and passed on to us without meaning to was: "Don't hope for anything too hard. Because the very second you're ready to taste the icing on the celebration cake, that's when you're going to drop your baton."

Mom saw the whole family staring at her—all but P.S., who was still splattering spaghetti sauce. She chattered on nervously. "It's not that I don't think you have a chance at going to Xavier," she told my brother, patting his hand. "But I don't want you to build your hopes up and get disappointed."

"Uh, Grace," Dad mumbled.

"*Yes,* Bill?" Mom said.

She gave him a look, and he stopped talking. He turned away hastily and started blotting spaghetti sauce off P.S.'s chin.

Logan stirred. "I'll just have to hope Mary Pat can pull me through."

Everyone at the table looked at him.

"You want *Mary Pat* to tutor you?" I asked, horrified.

He didn't answer.

"Hope for the best," Mom said briskly, "but expect the worst."

For some reason, tonight of all nights, it struck me as pretty good advice. I thought of myself out there on an empty playing field, flying over hurdles, and Logan applying to colleges with no hope of getting in. I thought of Dad's business problems and Mom's fifteen dogs and twenty-two cats. Only P.S. seemed to be as happy as a pig in spaghetti sauce.

All of a sudden P.S. sat straight up on his booster seat and covered his mouth with both hands. "I sick," he howled.

"What kind of sick?" Mom asked anxiously, starting out of her seat.

"My tummy!"

As Dad hauled my little brother off to the bathroom, Mom following behind, I sighed. Now we were at 100 percent. Our family's batons were falling all over the place.

8

Friday. Game day.

I had so many conflicted feelings—excitement, envy, misery—that I could hardly stand it. I didn't even want to go to the game, much less play team lackey. The first game had been tough enough, but that had been an unimportant game that didn't count in our ratings.

But homecoming. My stomach felt hollow.

Instead of rushing to the field early, I sat beside Sam in the Humane Society's outdoor visitors' pen. The two of us leaned against the wire fence with Max snuggled between us, his head on my leg. The pen was a shabby place that had been built by a kid working on his Eagle Scout badge, but Max couldn't have cared less. He was in bliss, his pump-handle tail wagging and his nose pushing against my hand as I petted him with the other one. He had no idea the axe was hanging over his wrinkled head.

Most of the dogs were kept on concrete slabs behind chain-link fences, and most of the cats were locked up in cages. Hundreds and hundreds of animals crowded the shelter; there were too many to keep them all. Right now thirty-eight dogs and fifty-six cats had twenty-one days to live.

That was our new countdown. We couldn't save them all, but we would work to reduce the numbers. After every execution we'd start all over again—an endless losing battle.

But this time was the worst. Today I had learned that Max was on the termination list. I begged Mom desperately to let me bring him home for a while. Just until we could find someone to adopt him.

I saw the answer in her sad eyes even before she shook her head. She had promised Dad. He had been so good about the menagerie we kept at home and the wildlife litters she raised to hand over to wildlife release experts. Half the time he could hardly find a spot to read his paper in. She couldn't ask him to take even one more animal.

But this was Max. My dog. She knew it, but she couldn't help. Surely we would find a home in time. Everyone would look, she promised me.

"Mom won't let me take him either," Sam said miserably. "Because of all our cats. She said a dog in the mix would be a mess."

"I have to leave for the game pretty soon," I said, not budging. Imagine a football game being the last place in the world I wanted to be.

"I suppose Cam-the-Awesome is looking forward to strutting his stuff on the field," Sam said. "It's embarrassing enough the way he struts it all over school."

"He may not be the nicest guy," I said, "but you must admit, he *does* pretty much own the school."

"What part of it? The stupid part?"

"Come on, Sam. The guy's a great quarterback. If the coach can find him a receiver and the team gets better, he'll probably get a football scholarship to college."

"Well, that's very nice and all," she said slowly, "but it doesn't really add up to much since he also throws food around the lunchroom and makes the ladies clean up after him and rags on everybody who's too shy to stand up to him. And he's so bad at schoolwork I'm surprised he even keeps his eligibility. He and Matt are both a year behind on math and science requirements, and here's Matt already resorting to cheating the first week of school. What do you want to bet Cam cheats, too? And the worst of it is they're not even slow learners, just lazy. Matt was in Perry's geometry class."

"Who *does* impress you?"

She turned her head and smiled at me. "You do, actually."

I felt my face turn red. "Why would I impress anybody?"

"You're smart, you're kind, and you don't ever hurt people, even the ones who hurt you. You care about animals." She grinned. "I even have a hunch you're a good football player."

Her hair was blowing in the warm breeze and she looked pretty, not just cute. I had a sudden thought that if she ever started wearing anything other than baggy jeans and sweatshirts, she might be something to see.

"Why would you think I'm a good football player?" I asked. "You've never seen me play."

"No," she agreed. "But I know you. You wouldn't want to play the game if you were terrible at it. That's why I hated to see you do the water boy thing when you really should be on the team. I say you belong on it."

"Coach seems to disagree. . . ."

"I don't think he's seen you, Joey. That's one of the things you're *not* good at. Showing off your assets. You have to have a good eye to see them. Like I do," she added with a little laugh as Max sat up and begged for food.

As I dug a dog biscuit out of my pocket, she murmured, "I hate to tell you this, Joey. . . ."

My stomach went into my throat. I put my hand on Max's head as he crunched away on his biscuit. Even before she said it, I knew what was coming.

"You're bringing Max to the game tonight, aren't you?" I said.

She nodded unhappily. "I'm really sorry, Joey, but we just have to find a home for him. If we don't—"

"Oh, sure," I said. My eyes burned and I hoped I wasn't going to embarrass myself by bursting into tears. "Bring him for sure, Sam. He needs a family of his own."

Sam had an agreement with the Humane Society where, under her mom's supervision, she could check animals out for special events where there would be lots of people. That way she might find homes for some of them. Even though they didn't allow pets inside the football stadium, she was planning to take several of the dogs on the termination list to tonight's game and put them in a pen outside the main entrance. If people signed up for adoption, they would have to go to the Society, fill out the application papers, and pay the adoption fees before taking their new pets home.

"I thought I'd dress him up like a Bulldogs' mascot," she said. "After all, he is a bulldog. He'll look so cute, he'll be sure to get a home."

"Yeah." I nodded slowly. The thought of not seeing him again was tough to take. "Maybe he'll bring us luck. Without Matt Burris as receiver, Tony Gilmore will be carrying the entire team on his skinny little shoulders. We'll need all the luck we can get."

Sam sniffled, and I noticed tears welling in her eyes. I put my arm across her shoulders, one pal to another, and said, "Just make sure somebody good gets him."

Max came scooting back onto my lap, looking up at me with that sorrowful look that only a bulldog can get on his mug.

Maybe by tonight he'd have found a home.

9

In the words of Woody Hayes, Ohio State's legendary coach: "There's nothing that cleanses your soul like getting the hell kicked out of you."

By all accounts, we were not far from a good cleansing.

The stadium lights were at full strength, the scoreboard was lit, and the snack bar was selling dozens of foot-long "Bull" dogs at two-fifty a pop. Our lousy band was on the field, led by Mr. Tucker. He was about sixty years old, had been a bandleader his whole adult life, and had the reputation of having never put together one good marching band. Ours was expertly chosen not to break his record: Half couldn't march and the other half couldn't play. The music gave the impression of several different tunes being played at the same time, which was frequently true. Marchers roved vaguely about the field, all of them in search of spots to call their own, while Mr. Tucker marched among them blasting away at a trumpet and trying to pull the discordant mess together.

Finally they got as close to success as was likely by somehow finding their way into a ragged, moving B formation, for "Bulldogs," marching triumphantly to laughs and fake cheers from the crowd who'd never believed they'd make it that far.

I spotted my brother carrying his sax along the bottom arc of the B, as lost as any marcher on the field. In the clarinet section, Perry Toomey looked to be marching sprightly. The plume on his hat flew merrily as he bopped his head to the music, no doubt playing his clarinet with trills and finesse and finding his way through the formations like he did everything else—perfectly.

Meanwhile cheerleaders waved their pompoms, the people in the stands yelled, and more fans poured in through the turnstile. As the band left the field, I rushed to set up the water bottles, the Gatorade tank, and some paper cups. Then I lined up the medical supplies.

By this time the Great Receiver would have pulled on his red home jersey, white pants, and shoulder pads. He'd be walking around in his football cleats now, carrying his helmet, with his mind on the game. "Don't try to be a hero out there," he'd be telling himself. "Just execute, execute, execute. Fundamentals. Run crisp routes. Run hard even when you're a decoy. Catch the ball before you run with it. Push off your blocks. Be smart." He'd be going over the plays, though, of course, he'd already know them backward and forward.

The coach would be settling the team down now, giving his pre-game pep talk and notes. When he finished, all the players would put their hands together and yell "Bulldogs! Yeah!"

The GR would take his place in the line, ready to run onto the field.

"You can get the ice from the refreshment stand now, Joey."

"Huh?" I blinked and saw Karen Harris standing in front of me, wearing her Bulldog's cap, white trainer's skirt, and red polo shirt. "Oh, right." I trudged across the field and through the chain-link door opposite the refreshment booth. People in the bleachers were stomping, holding up signs, and following the cheerleaders in a rousing cheer.

I waited for the ice, staring through the turnstile where I could see Sam, her mom, Kathy, and her aunt Betty, watching over the pen of Humane Society dogs. A crowd was milling around the pen, pointing at Max's Bulldog outfit and laughing.

He was wearing red baby socks with the bottoms cut out, a tiny cut-off Bulldogs T-shirt, and red and white ribbons tied to his collar and around the base of his tail. The animals all trotted around, fur blowing, ears alert, looking revved and ready for action.

By the time I went back inside the stadium, the band had finished lining up on the bleacher. Drums were thumping, getting louder and faster by the minute, the brass was trumpeting a fight song, and the cheerleaders were forming a tunnel by the home team's entrance. I couldn't help noticing Nancy Frazier and Ashley Parker waving their pompoms, looking good in red-and-white short skirts. I could just imagine Sam rolling her eyes and saying something like, "So they've got legs. Too amazing."

The stands suddenly roared. Cam came running through the cheerleaders' tunnel amid the madly waving pompoms, carrying his helmet so his face and blond hair would show. The rest of the team wore theirs, charging behind him, heads down like rampaging bulls, followed by the coaches. Cam ran straighter than the rest, head up, looking like a true star.

The crowd cheered louder, feet stamping, waving "Bull" dogs on sticks, pompoms, and plastic wiggle lights. The home team tore across the field and then formed a line while the visiting Tigers ran out.

Watching both teams stand respectfully during a discordant rendition of "The Star-Spangled Banner," I knew I'd have paid anything to be out there on the field.

In the scattered applause after the anthem, a sudden loud cheer went up. I followed the crowd's attention and saw Max trotting onto the field alongside Nancy Frazier, his wrinkled head raised proudly, his red and white ribbons streaming in the night air. He strutted proudly as if he knew the whistles and cheers were for him. The laughs were, too.

The laughs grew louder when Max plunked down midfield, having gone as far as he wanted to go, and Nancy tried to pick him up and failed. Cheers replaced the laughter when a male cheerleader came over and carried him to the sidelines, where the other cheerleaders formed an admiring circle around him. Max was in. A set of red socks and a T-shirt and the dog I loved had become part of the loop. The traitor never once looked my way as I stood by the water barrel with the other three hydration therapists: Daphne Howard, Britton Reese, and Dave Louden.

"We got us a *mascot, yeah!*" some guy bellowed among the hoots and shouts.

The refs beckoned co-captains Cam and Brady and the Tigers' co-captains onto the field for the coin toss. Ice water trickled into my stomach. I cheered with the rest when we won with a heads' call and elected to receive. Cam walked off regally, blond head shining in the overhead lights.

"You'd think he personally told the coin which way to land," I muttered.

"What?" Daphne Howard snapped, glaring at me as she grabbed a water bottle from the ice in case Cam needed a pre-game swig.

"I said Cam has supernatural abilities," I said. "He made that coin land heads up."

Her indignant look faded to awe. "Wow. You really think so?"

"Absolutely. If you don't believe me, ask him."

Not being in the loop either, she avoided my eyes. Cam wouldn't give her the time of day, much less enter into a conversation about the paranormal. She wasn't rich enough or self-confident enough, nor did she meet the sublime beauty requirements dictated by the loop's taste.

The kick-off return team lined up. Tony Gilmore caught the ball at the ten-yard line and streaked away from the Tigers' major speed merchant, who got there before the slower, bulkier guys. Tony tried to run up the middle and bounced off a couple of would-be tacklers, looking like a feisty rat ricocheting off two meaty gorillas. Then, with Ricardo Gonzalez blocking another attack, he broke toward the sidelines and turned upfield for a run to the forty-five yard line. He might have taken it all the way but for a saving tackle by the Tigers' kicker.

"*Yeah!*" I yelled, almost colliding with Roddy Doogan, who thudded past me on his way to the field, his thick stomach jostling under his jersey.

Roddy's jersey didn't stay clean for long. On the first play in the series, he lost a one-on-one contest with a charging linebacker, skidded facedown on the field, and sat up chewing grass. Next play, Melvin Barr ground out three yards. Then Cam tried to throw over the middle to Brian Freeman at tight end, but a tall Tigers' linebacker knocked it down, and we had to kick.

Our defense held them, and they had to kick to us.

On the first play, Tony shot up the center only to be creamed by a two-hundred-pound tackle. A pass to Andy Doogan, Roddy's younger brother, fell flat, but Tony nailed a first down when Cam confused the Tigers with a fake handoff to Melvin. It became too clear too quick that Melvin and Tony were the only real offensive weapons we had working.

I was dying to be out there, aching to be another weapon in the Bulldogs' arsenal. I wasn't quick off the mark, but after the first few steps, my long legs could run circles around anybody on our team.

Just give me the chance.

On first and ten, Tony ran off-tackle with a halfback sweep to the right. But the Tigers keyed on him so tight he couldn't tie his shoelace without being tackled. He was lucky to gain a total of two yards. We lost a yard next play when the defense penetrated and Cam was forced to fall on the ball. On third and long, the play was designed as a quick out to Tommy Brink, who was open in the flat.

Cam hesitated, then drew back his arm to throw.

The team flinched and half the guys on the sidelines closed their eyes, expecting to see the same trampoline act they'd seen in practice. Coach Stanley, the receiver coach, had both hands flat on his hair like he was trying to keep the top of his head on.

"Did anybody see if Tommy stuck his hands in that bucket of grease he carries around with him?" Brady growled.

Nobody laughed.

Dancing backward with the ball, Cam didn't look that happy either. At the last second, with the defensive line almost on top of him, he changed his mind and fired over the middle to Brian Freeman, who was in double coverage and not expecting the pass. The blocking was less than perfect, and the throw was hurried and off its mark. Still, the ball was catchable.

Brian—Mr. Freeze himself—dropped it.

Cam headed for the sidelines with the groaning crowd in shock and both coaches waiting for him. Miller had first pecking rights.

"You do realize Tommy was wide open?" the Iron Jaw growled. "Why the hell didn't you throw to him?"

"Crap," Brady groaned, looking at Tommy, who came steaming off the field, jerked his helmet off, and glared at Cam.

"Thanks, pal! Always glad to get your respect!" Tommy snapped.

"Earn it and you'll get it!" Cam shot back.

"One more word," warned the Iron Jaw, "and you're both out of the game. I've got a backup quarterback, and my aunt would make a better receiver."

Their mouths flew open, but no words came out. The Coach waited, stony-faced, and then stalked away.

The only thing the disappointed Bulldog fans understood was that the punt team was coming onto the field.

Pale with rage, Cam turned on me. "Can't you even hand out water, you idiot? Or maybe you've got a bet on the other team and want me dehydrated? Let me make it clear that I want water waiting for me if I even *look* like I'm starting toward the sidelines!"

All this, while Daphne was waiting hopefully, holding a bottle of water right in front of him. But Cam wanted the water from me for some reason. Without a word I yanked a bottle from the ice bucket and held it out. He jerked it from my hand and plunked down on the bench beside Roddy Doogan.

After that I had to make sure that the second Cam so much as glanced at the sidelines there was a bottle of water with his name on it. His bitter grin told me that tormenting me was his only source of amusement tonight.

When I wasn't hustling water for Cam or the rest of the team, Karen Harris was calling for bandages and ice. Then Melvin Barr got a cramp and needed someone to stretch his legs. Karen tended to Melvin and pointed me over to Tony with a cold pack for his cheek. Looking closely, I saw the huge bruise spreading across his dark skin.

"Bad one," I said, pressing the ice pack gently against his face.

"I've had worse," he grinned, trying not to flinch.

It started to rain, a drenching, warm rain that soaked the field and turned dirt to mud. I soon found myself on my hands and knees scraping mud from cleats. All the time I was groaning inside. I could help the Bulldogs; I knew I could. Unfortunately I was the only one who knew it.

On the next possession, we lost our second wide receiver, Wayne Yeager, to a twisted ankle. More bandages and ice were needed. Karen went back to the locker room with Wayne. His ankle would be all right, but just to be on the safe side, he would miss the rest of the game.

"Will you stretch my legs already?" Melvin grumped.

I jumped and mumbled, "Sorry." I'd been thinking about the Great Receiver suddenly getting tapped by the coach and running onto the field to huge cheers.

The pattern of the game was now set. Neither team had much of an offense, but both played solid defense. From here on it would be a struggle for field position, relying on special teams to put points on the board.

Between rain and sweat, Tony's muscled but under-sized body looked like it belonged to a drowned muskrat. Not only was he the key running back, he was also on kick-off and punt returns. All this for zero points. He, Melvin, and Brian represented most of our offense, and all were tiring, Tony in particular.

By now Cam was throwing to Tommy Brink, and rain

had not improved Tommy's receptions. If the Cirque du Soleil had been in town, there would have been a high cash offer for use of his chest as a trampoline, not to speak of soccer teams bidding for his head.

It was close to halftime, and nobody wanted to give the other team a last-minute score. If we could just hold them until the half, then maybe our team could rally.

"HOLD THE BALL!" Coach Miller suddenly bellowed. "DON'T PASS IT!"

Arms deep in melting ice, I looked up wildly from the drink barrel to see Cam in his throwing stance, keying in on Tommy, who was in the clear and triumphantly waving for the pass. The coach's yell came a second too late. Cam had already released the ball.

The air left my lungs and the coach uttered a word he would never use in a classroom, as Cam's rather timid pass traveled directly into what should have been Tommy's arms. Instead of catching it, Tommy chest-butted the ball cleanly into the hands of the Tigers' middle linebacker.

A roar of *NOOOOOOOOO* came from the crowd as the linebacker streaked thirty yards down the sideline with the ball tucked under his arm. When he crossed into the end zone, a tuba burped out an "oops" kind of sound and time ran out. That was the moment I knew we'd lost the game. I felt it in my gut.

We left for the locker room with most heads hanging, leaving the band to straggle back onto the wet field, sounding worse than in its pre-game disaster. With the locker room closed against the sound, Coach Miller ordered every player to take a seat. Then he looked down at his clipboard and began talking. Faces got longer and redder with every note.

"Don't go back out there with your tails between your legs," he concluded. "It isn't dignified. And don't go out there emotional. Think about how each of you specifically can get cleaner and better. Our offensive line is not holding our blocks. Anticipate, engage, and hold! You're getting beat off the ball. And we've got to do a better job at picking up those blitzes. If there's one thing that can kill us, it's missing a blitz. Tony, Melvin, you're both doing all you can out there. If we can create a few holes for you, we'll get some points on the board. We're playing great defensive ball. Let's see if we can get a few turnovers. Those guys out there are not bigger or stronger than we are, but right now they're playing smarter than we are. Let's turn that around and go get 'em!"

If anyone was listening, you couldn't tell by the way the Bulldogs dragged themselves back onto the field after the half and played ball like losers, with four turnovers, eight of thirty passing, and a beat-up defense. They limped back into the locker room after a walloping loss of 31-0, leaving a three-quarters empty stadium behind them. Most of the crowd had left before the last quarter had even begun.

The cheerleaders were giving a cheer to salute the team's efforts, but their voices sounded as shrill as bats. Max had disappeared from the squad, maybe having proven himself unlucky enough to sour them on the whole idea of having a mascot.

Cam was still standing midfield in a red-faced daze, the

last player to leave the field. He had a football clenched tightly in his hand, looking like he'd like to cream somebody, when suddenly a voice in the stands yelled down at him.

"Hey, Supercam! You weren't such a showboat out there tonight! What happened, bighead?"

I could hardly believe my eyes. *Perry Toomey?* Yet there he was, standing on top of a bleacher and buzzing Cam a nasty raspberry.

If there was a wrong thing to say and a wrong time to say it, Perry had found it. In Cam's hand, a football could turn into a cannonball. Sure enough, he turned and flung the ball as hard as he could, directly at Perry's pointy little head. I was about halfway between the two of them, my arms full of medical supplies.

Perry's mental reflexes might be great, but physically he was no match for Cam. He was getting ready to take a big one, and it wasn't for the team.

I went up for the ball. Cannonball or not, I brought the football in clean, tossed it into an equipment bag, then leaned down to pick up the medical kit I'd just dropped. By then Cam was halfway to the locker room, and Perry had scrambled from the bleachers and disappeared into the crowd that was leaving the stands.

"Nice catch, Joey."

I turned around to see Coach Miller standing only a few feet away. A lump formed in my throat. I couldn't say a word.

He looked at me under raised eyebrows. "I remember you tried out for the team."

"Yeah," I managed to croak. "I was pretty bad."

"That wasn't exactly an easy catch you just made."

"Well, thanks." I turned toward the refreshment cart and stumbled, knowing he was standing there, looking at me. I cursed myself silently as the other hydration therapists and I loaded the cart. Karen, Daphne, and Britton drove off in the cart, while Dave and I trotted back to the locker room.

Good job, Joey, I groaned to myself. Once again you managed to seize failure from the jaws of a small piece of success. Really fine work.

The team gathered on the benches and looked at Coach Miller, who seemed lost in thought and calmer than he had been during halftime.

"No practice on Monday, guys," the coach said. "Let's take the day to regroup and lick our wounds. Don't worry, there's always another game. We've got a lot of talent on this team. It's my fault if I don't use it to the best advantage."

After the team showered, dressed, and trudged out to the parking lot, I collected the last of the wet towels and figured I was done for the night. Sam would be waiting for me, and I could find out who had adopted Max. He had sure looked on top of it tonight, running alongside Nancy in his stupid mascot outfit. I grinned, remembering Nancy struggling to lift him. Still, the idea of his being adopted . . .

"*Hey, Eastland!*"

The voice came from behind me. When I wheeled

around, a football was coming at me high and hard, down a row of lockers.

It was a zinger, straight at my head.

I caught it one-handed, wet towels and all. Coach was standing at the end of the row from where he'd launched the ball.

He was a hefty guy, built more like an offensive tackle than a quarterback, but even if I didn't already know he had been a star QB at State, I would have suspected it now. There wasn't any doubt that he could still throw a football. My hand stung.

"So it wasn't an accident," he said. He sat down on a long bench and looked at me as if he'd never seen me before tonight. "Not bad for a hydration therapist." He grinned a little. "Mrs. Cunningham told me you were determined not to quit your job with the team. She said you were pretty intense about it. I'm starting to understand why."

"Uh . . ."

He studied me thoughtfully, and I figured he was remembering the details of my lousy tryout—until he said, "Next time, remember to use two hands to catch a football, whether you think you need 'em or not. A football is always better caught in two hands, not one, if you get that opportunity. Okay?"

"Yes sir."

"Where did you learn to catch like that?" the coach went on.

"I used to play flag football, and my dad and I throw in

the park. My brother and I have a kind of pitch-and-catch game we do while we're stocking shelves at Dad's store."

"Yeah?" The coach looked interested. "Does your brother play any kind of ball?"

I thought of Logan and laughed. "Nope, he can't even really catch paint buckets very well. He'd rather hurl stuff at me. And he hates exercise. He's in the band, but hates to march."

"Too bad. You look like you work out. Do you?"

"After practice, yeah. And I run at night."

"You pretty fast?"

I shrugged. "Fast enough after three steps." My heart began to gallop.

Coach's face was unreadable. He never took his eyes off me. "How about if I see you at practice on Monday, Joey? Right after class."

"I thought there wasn't any . . ."

"Just you," Coach Miller said and then added almost to himself, "and probably Cam."

I swallowed hard and nodded.

"Funny thing is, I had a note on your tryout. You were the last man cut."

Astonished, I stared at him. "I was awful. I dropped everything and my running was the pits."

"Yeah, but I thought I saw something. Should have trusted my instincts."

Speechlessly, I stood rooted, expecting him to come to his senses any second.

"Right then." He was gone, leaving me to wander around in the empty locker room, up one row and down the next. I wasn't even aware that I was still carrying an armload of wet towels until I looked down and saw both hands hanging onto them, white-knuckled from gripping too hard. I stuck them in the hamper, then walked outside the locker room into a new world. The field lights were dimming and the stands were almost empty. Parent volunteers were cleaning the snack bar and preparing to close it down. All was quiet except for my pounding heart.

Had I really just been invited to try out for the team? I tried to shake it off. There had to be some mistake.

You were the last man cut. It echoed over and over in my mind.

Past the turnstile, I saw Sam leaning against a buckeye tree, waiting for me, leash in hand. Max was attached to it, and when I jogged over to the tree, he leaped up at me like a puppy. Not bad for a dog that close to the ground and one who hated any kind of exertion. Especially since he'd had a major workout tonight.

"Did anyone sign up to adopt him?"

"In a way. He got sort of a temporary home." She grinned at me. "During the game, my mom called your mom on her cell. And guess what? Your mom checked with your dad and they agreed he could stay with you. Just for the season. He's the Bulldogs' official mascot now." Her face fell a little. "But after the season ends, we'll have to find him a home. Still, he's got a stay of execution."

"Really?" I couldn't stop grinning. "I can't believe it. This, on top of the coach."

"The coach? What about him?"

"He . . ." I felt myself blushing. "He saw me catch a

ball. Then, in the locker room, he threw me another and asked me a few questions. He's scheduled a special practice for me. I think it may be a tryout. Can you believe it?"

She opened her mouth, but seemed to have trouble saying anything. Standing there beaming at me, she finally choked out, "That's wonderful, Joey. I'm so happy for you! I really am!"

"Well, it's not set that I'll make the team," I said uncomfortably, not wanting to get her hopes up.

"I think you will," she said firmly. Her eyes were damp for the second time in one day. She blinked the tears away.

"What if I screw up the tryout?"

"Be positive, Joey," she begged. "You don't have to be perfect. Coach Miller is a very intelligent man. Just look at what a good Spanish teacher he is."

"I take French," I reminded her.

"Take my word for it, he's terrific. He'll see how good you are. I just know it!"

"Unfortunately, teaching Spanish doesn't have much to do with being a good coach—though actually he's that, too. I'll just have to do my best and hope. And I get Max, too."

A horn honked long and hard from the parking lot.

Sam's hand flew over her mouth. "Mary Pat! I completely forgot. She's . . . uh, listen, you want to go for a hamburger?"

I laughed. "It better be somewhere we can take a dog."

"Logan and Mary Pat are waiting for us in the parking lot. I can't believe I forgot."

We started walking. "I guess she'll be driving."

She rolled her eyes at me. "You think she'd let him drive her car? Come on, we've kept them waiting and Logan's hungry. He's *really* hungry. Wait till they hear!"

"She's got a new sports car, you know. We'll be scrunched up together in that little backseat."

Sam smiled. "I don't mind. Come on!"

10

Sam and I sat on one side of the booth. Opposite us Mary Pat and Logan pored over a menu together. Logan had that anxious look he got when deciding about food, something akin to how I probably looked around several cheerleaders in short skirts.

I was still in a dream, waiting for my alarm to ring and wake me up, minus both my dog and my tryout.

Sam grinned at me. "It's real."

The waitress appeared, pad in hand. "Okay. What will we have here?"

Logan's mouth opened.

"I'm thinking ten, maybe fifteen, French fries for you, Logan," Mary Pat said quickly. "So we'll have to split an order of fries." She turned to the waitress. "And he'll have . . . let's see, a nice plain hamburger with half a bun."

"Half a bun," Logan groaned, his face falling.

She smiled at him kindly. "You already ate half a hot dog from the snack bar."

"Every other member of the band ate a lot more than half a dog. Popcorn was flying on all sides of me; pizza was in my face; ice cream . . . I tell you, I'm seriously hungry. At least let me have a full bun."

"Don't bring the other half to the table, please," Mary Pat warned the waitress. "He'd eat it." She looked unhappily at Logan. "Believe me, honey, I understand how hard diets are. I practically live on one. Now let's see. What will I have?" She bent her head and studied the combo specials.

The waitress looked back at Logan. "What to drink?"

Mary Pat looked up and mouthed, *Diet Coke,* then smiled sympathetically when Logan moaned about missing his usual shake. "And I'll have . . . let's see. Right, I'll have the chiliburger combo and the chocolate shake. Oh, the combo comes with fries? Oh, well, just bring them. I haven't eaten much today. Thanks so much!"

Sam and I ordered burgers, fries, and shakes, plus an extra burger for Max. When the food came, I cut Max's burger up and took it out to him before touching my own. I wasn't all that hungry. My stomach was full of butterflies.

"Even the dog got a whole bun," Logan complained as I left for the car, with Mary Pat reminding me to stay until Max ate his food, to make sure he didn't slobber on her upholstery.

With his appetite, that didn't take long. I came back inside and slipped into the booth. Across from me Logan was nibbling dejectedly at his fifteen fries and small burger, while Mary Pat beamed at me and chewed a mouthful of chiliburger. Her half order of Logan's fries was gone and she was well into her own.

"I think it's so cool that you're getting the tryout, Joey," she smiled, after washing down the chiliburger with a long gulp of her shake. "I know you'll be wonderful!"

"I may be lousy," I mumbled. "I'd just as soon we kept it to ourselves."

"Well, honey, everyone's going to know." She pumped catsup onto her fries. "You'll be trying out right there on the field. How can you hide it?"

I grimaced, realizing she was right. There would be no way to keep it a secret if I fell flat on my face.

"Joey will do just fine," Sam said. I'd seen those little pink spots on her cheeks before, usually at the Society, when a mistreated dog came in. They meant she was seriously ticked.

"I *know* he'll be fine!" Mary Pat exclaimed. "I think he'll be absolutely wonderful! I, for one, will be right there watching. I wouldn't miss it! You're going to be there, aren't you, Sam?"

"If Joey wants me to be there," Sam said firmly.

"Well, he does, don't you, honey?"

I nodded. Sure, why not? In fact, why not put it in the papers? The more the merrier, to watch me fall on my butt. For that was what I suddenly felt sure was going to happen.

"I wish Logan were into sports." Mary Pat sighed. "Keeps you in shape. That reminds me, honey, you need to exercise while you're dieting. I know you hate exercise now, but you'll grow to love it. When we're married and living in Pittsburgh, I'll make sure you go to the gym at least four nights a week."

"*Pittsburgh?*" Sam and I said at the same time.

It caught up to Logan a second later. *"Pittsburgh?"* He stared at her in shock.

"My uncle Mike's got a veterinary practice there." Mary Pat smiled at him like she'd just handed him a present. "You'll go into practice with him, and when he retires, you'll take over. You can easily make over six figures there. I'll be a lawyer, of course, so we'll have no trouble at all supporting four children."

"Four kids?" he repeated. *"Pittsburgh? Uncle Mike?"*

"I just thought of it the other day. I didn't mention it to you because you need to focus on the here and now. No use dreaming of a veterinary practice until you improve that SAT score. No, better just to study, study, study."

"Right," my brother said dully.

"And I'll be with you all the way! There's nothing I love more than helping to mold you, honey. Who wants some guy who's all put together? With you, I'm like a sculptress with a pile of wet, lumpy clay, looking to make a masterpiece!"

Logan was too stunned to speak. He watched the rest of us wolf down our food.

Mary Pat smiled at Sam and me. "By the way, are you two dating now? Is it official?"

Sam turned red, and I shook my head. "Not really," Sam said. "We're just friends," I said at the same time. Sam went redder than ever.

"Pity." Mary Pat sighed. "You make a really good couple. If you want to date other people, you should avoid being seen together too much or they'll think you're hands-off. Well, it's getting late! Everybody up, let me check you for crumbs before you get in the car."

Back at home, I filled a water bowl for Max, and we headed upstairs. As I changed into my pj's, I kept imagining dropping balls, tripping over tiny holes in the ground, overrunning the ball, underrunning the ball, losing the ball in the sun, letting balls squirt out of my hands like they were gushing through oil slicks. Seeing me in action, the coach might say, "Sorry, Joey, I was wrong. Your true vocation is passing out water bottles, after all."

Max, always empathetic, looked worried. He lay stretched out close by the bunk beds with his jowls resting on his front legs and his pudgy paws inched out in front, never taking his eyes off me.

"Okay," I said, looking around the room. "You've visited here before, so you know the ropes. No chewing shoes, no stealing socks." I shook my finger in his face. "No making any messes. Of *any kind*. And sleeping on my bed . . . is definitely allowed."

I took off his shirt, socks, and ribbons and gave him a boost up to my upper bunk. He hunkered down happily, and I crawled in beside him. As usual he was taking up more than his share of the bed.

I grinned. It was great to have my dog with me.

11

"Of course, I know who you are!" Mom said brightly into the phone on Sunday afternoon. "Joey always talks about how smart you are!" Pause. "Yes, I think I knew you were also a musician. . . . oh, and a chess player. And, my goodness, really? You speak five languages, too? What would they . . . ? Oh, sorry, Perry, Joey's grabbing the phone. Nice talking to you!"

"Hi, Joey," Perry said in pleased tones. "Very nice of you to mention me to your mom. If she wants to know, besides English, I speak Italian, Russian, Chinese, and Spanish. Of course, I've also studied Latin, but few really speak that anymore, so—"

He waited patiently while I repeated them all to Mom, who was impressed. Then he wanted me to mention his solar-powered helicopter. Finally he got to the point and told me that Mrs. Cunningham had called a meeting with our group Monday morning before class.

"Well, see you then, Joey. I'll probably be texting or e-mailing any special messages as we go along. By the way, have you been studying the DNA charts for our lab project? I want to make sure we're both prepared for what's ahead."

"I'll hop to it, chief." Most of our labs, including dissections, were done virtually on individual computers. But there was also a cooperative DNA study, where we would collect specimens and eventually use the local facilities of Bioscope Systems to track DNA strands and make comparisons to other DNA.

"I want you to know genes and chromosomes backward," he said.

"Okay. I'll cover that, and would you cover them forward?"

"Always the clown," Perry said indulgently. "I'll see you at seven A.M. Terrible hour, isn't it? I like to spend that hour every day reviewing for my upcoming classes."

"They'll pickle his brain one day" I said, hanging up. "Probably while he's still alive."

He had left me no option on anything. Not only would I have to get up an hour earlier, but this afternoon I would be stuck studying scientific terms. But first a game of Frisbee, if Max would get off his lazy butt. Luckily he was agreeable, so long as I threw it close and low and wasn't in any hurry to get it back.

At seven the next morning, Mrs. C. was the first one in her classroom, armed with reams of printed papers and on full adrenaline surge. "I have decided to meet with you before school twice a week," she said. "Mondays and Thursdays. One of our members is unable to make after-school meetings." She looked directly at me. "Joey Eastland, thank the fellow members of your team for accommodating this inconvenience."

All but Sam stared my way, their slight frowns signifying that I had cost them an hour of sleep twice weekly. Perry looked especially peeved, seeming to feel that he should have been privy to my schedule conflicts.

"Why didn't you tell me you were the one who caused her to change our meeting time?" he whispered.

"How did I know she changed it because of me?" I hissed back. Sam kept her eyes down, examining the reference material Mrs. C. had handed out.

"Eastland?"

"Um, thanks," I mumbled to my disgruntled classmates. I looked down at my own stack of paper.

We would be studying differences and similarities of life in each region of the world. Perry's beginning assignment was to use preserved artifacts to show how various cultures had historically affected one another. Sam meanwhile would find examples of worldwide cultural engagement and assimilation, as opposed to cultural imperialism.

"It's important," Mrs. C. said, "to engage with the world without relinquishing our own individuality or changing others' uniqueness."

"Example, please," Perry said importantly.

"Foreign films come to mind. It happens that the French government does not favor its people watching American films, unless they re-dub them to reflect local culture. However many other countries watch our films more than their own. Does this have cultural impact?"

Perry nodded vigorously, his mouth open, his neck straining over the top of his baby blue-and-white plaid pullover as he stretched in his seat, trying to get her attention. He looked as if he had come to class in his sister's pajama top.

Before he could answer, she continued: "You bet it does! Many foreign audiences dress like our stars and imitate lifestyles they see on the screen, losing pieces of their own culture in the process. Whereas France retains much of its unique nature."

Sam looked up from her notes. "So cultural assimilation would be engaging with each other without destroying each other's customs and ways? And cultural imperialism does the opposite?"

Mrs. Cunningham nodded. "Very good. Now let's see. Yes, next we come to Joseph Eastland." Mrs. C. turned her full attention on me. "I thought we might start you with a study of global sports, Eastland," she said, her mouth twitching slightly.

Perry squirmed in his seat.

"Yes, Perry Toomey? Do you perhaps need to use the facilities?"

Perry blushed, but there were no titters. Samantha was not a titterer and neither were the two art students, who did not look up from their individual doodlings. Being tittered at so much myself had left me with no taste for it either.

Under her fierce gaze, he mumbled, "I . . . I was . . . you mean . . . well, I was wondering. Is that all he's doing? Just *sports*?"

Her eyebrows arched fiercely. "You wouldn't be insinuating that I have favorites in this class, Mr. Toomey?"

"Oh! Oh, no ma' am! Not at all, I just—"

"Excellent," she murmured, cutting him off at the pass.

"You all will work hard in this project, none spared." She looked at me. "Please examine the historical roots of sports, starting back about five thousand years ago, in the Egyptian, Roman, and Greek cultures. I will want you to trace how sports have affected international relationships through history, Eastland."

She turned to her project artists, Kelsey Magnum and Ted Wyatt. "I'll want you two to read all the material, too, and start dreaming your images."

Kelsey looked up. "I'm seeing transparent watercolors. Multicultural people celebrating together." She smiled vaguely.

Kelsey would have stood out in any school. She had straight hair and no makeup, was usually paint-splotched and dressed absentmindedly in mismatched clothes. And yet she was also tall and willowy, blonde and beautiful; she really didn't need to think about how she looked. She also played the violin and sang so well that she occasionally performed small roles in the local opera. But though she could have had a date with any boy in school, loop or no loop, she walked alone and carried her own books, her mind on her music and art. She never seemed nervous, and she had more self-confidence than anyone I knew, even Cam. If only I had what she had, I could give a good tryout with *nine* schools watching.

Mrs. C. was looking at Ted Wyatt. "Cartoons would be lovely, with those wonderful creatures of yours. I was thinking of that tree spirit thing, its branches spreading out over the world. What was his name?"

"Stump," Perry said, beating Ted to the punch.

"Sure, we could use him." Ted nodded, grinning shyly. He was an animation artist, already well known in our area for a recent environmental campaign he'd done featuring a giant oak tree named Stump. As far as I knew, Ted didn't date either, but then he didn't have Kelsey's physical attributes. His ears stuck out, his nose was hooked, and he had an acne problem. And that was just for starters.

Mrs. C. gave Ted a warm smile. "We are in your hands most of all, Ted Wyatt," she said. "We will need those happy images of yours to make our friends around the world smile and laugh. One of our projects will be an animated film. Perhaps you and Kelsey can put your heads together and decide how best to integrate your different styles."

She fell silent for a moment, looking at the five of us over the rims of her glasses. Perched on the edge of her desk, she sat with a straight back and raised head, looking very fine in a black pants suit, white blouse, and jade-green necklace, her black hair pulled firmly back in its usual bun. Her eyes were dark and shining, her mahogany-colored skin glowing.

"I think we have the makings of something wonderful here," she began, then stopped speaking. A sudden, thick silence lowered itself on my head. When I looked up, Mrs. C. was no longer looking full of idealistic hopes. She was frowning directly at me.

"Eastland, you with us this morning?"

She had caught me daydreaming about the football tryout after school.

"When you come here from now on," she said,

"remember this is *my* time—time I scheduled to convenience you, Eastland. So please be accountable."

"Yes ma'am." Luckily the bell rang, or I might have fallen to my knees begging for forgiveness.

"Fine. All right, we are finished here, ladies and gentlemen. We will meet again on Thursday, same time, with something to show me, please. Y'all have a nice day now. I'll see some of you in class later."

Perry Toomey put a plate of home-baked cookies on her desk as he left. "My mom sent these. Chocolate chips and nuts."

"My children will rise up and bless her," Mrs. C. said with her great laugh. "Their mama doesn't bake or sew, poor little hungry ragged lambs."

As I was reaching the door, I looked back to see her crooking her finger at me and I came back to her desk. What power the woman had! I had actually *felt* her crooking that finger.

"I hear you have a special practice today, Eastland. Good luck with it."

My mouth dropped open. "How did you—?"

"I hear things." She grinned at me, showing some major teeth. "Like I said, good luck."

Sam was waiting for me in the hall. "What did she want?"

"She heard about the football tryout."

"*What*? How on Earth . . . ?"

"They know in the next galaxy," I said, resigned to a mob scene at the football field.

"Joey, are you sure you want me to come?"

81

"I may need first aid afterward. I know I'll need a friend."

She let out her breath. "I'll be there. And Joey . . . just remember one thing. The coach already knows what he knows."

Glassy-eyed, I stared at her. "What does *that* mean?"

"It means try to take it a little easier." She put her hand on my shoulder and looked into my eyes. "I think your real tryout was in the locker room."

But moving down the hallway beside her, I thought of Cam and felt myself start to trip over my own feet. He hadn't seen me catch that ball in the locker room or on the field. He thought I was the biggest loser he'd ever seen. And this afternoon he would be throwing to me.

"Don't get nervous now, Eastland. We know how you shrivel under pressure. We don't want you making an idiot of yourself again."

I knew the voice. My stomach did a nosedive. I looked up to see Cam by himself for once.

"You're coming to the tryout then?" I croaked.

He walked closer, completely ignoring Sam beside me. He got so close in my face I could have counted his eyelashes. "I wouldn't miss it for a seat on the fifty-yard line at the Super Bowl," he said, showing his teeth in a sharp smile. "I'm going to make you earn every catch. I'm going to bruise your hands and make you dive. I don't know how you finagled this second chance tryout, but you ain't using me, understand? People don't use Cam McKey." He winked at me and added meaningfully, "I'll see you on the field."

He moved on, leaving me trembling and Sam clutching my hand so hard that her nails dug into my palm.

"Joey? You okay? He's just a creep; don't you dare let him get to you!"

I took back my hand. Not because I didn't want her holding it. I just didn't want her to feel me shaking.

"Yeah," I mumbled, not looking at her. "Okay."

"Oh, Joey," she said miserably. "You're worth ten of him. You just don't know it."

I didn't say anything else. Neither did she. We just walked.

12

There was a definite smell of blood in the air. Mine. The word had gotten out that Cam was going to demolish me.

By the time Advanced Placement U.S. history, my last class, was over, my insides were jumping. It was time.

I headed straight to the locker room and changed into a practice jersey, athletic shorts, and cleats. When I came out, the bleachers were filling up and Cam was already on the field, throwing to Coach Stanley.

Desperately, I drew myself taller and lifted my head, trying to be the Great Receiver. But pretending to be him was a lot easier when I was lying in bed or daydreaming in a class or at Dad's store than when I was walking onto a field in front of a mob of people, most of whom were probably hoping to see me knocked on my butt. ("Pul-eeze, Joey," Sam would say if she knew what I was thinking. "Most of them would be *for* you, not *against* you!")

Coach Miller was late. Maybe he had changed his mind, I thought wildly. I wondered whether I should just turn around and go back into the locker room. But no, Coach Stanley was here. Something was happening.

My stomach turned to ice as I suddenly saw the coach coming down the little hill that led from the athletic office to the field. He had changed to sweats and a pullover and was wearing a whistle around his neck. Feeling all eyes turn to me, I started trembling from head to toe. Especially my legs and my hands, the two things I needed most. My palms were dripping with sweat, making them perfect for catching. Great.

"Hey, Joey," the coach said, coming onto the field and motioning Cam over. He took the ball from him and flipped it to me. I grabbed it with shaky, sweaty hands and held on like it was a greased pig.

Cam sneered and glanced toward the stands. A hoot of laughter went up.

The coach looked at me. "Take two laps, Eastland. And get the attitude out of you."

"Me? Attitude?" I couldn't believe he was talking to me.

"Yeah, you. There're all kinds, you know." He pointed at the field and said, "Hit it."

Cam watched me head for the track, smirking until the coach turned to him.

"You, too."

"Come *on*," Cam said, as if the coach was pouring honey over him and getting ready to unlock the ants.

"Get out there, both of you! *Move it!*"

Cam said a word the coach didn't like, but he moved. So did I. Pretty soon he was following me around the track. I figured that any second he'd catch up, but when I finally glanced back, he was about twenty yards behind and losing ground. My longer stride continued to put distance between us. When we finished the second lap, he was almost fifty yards back.

Coach Stanley came onto the field. As receiver coach, he would be the one training the new wide receiver.

"Good stride, Eastland. How are you on the takeoff?"

"I'm not much of a sprinter. I could use some help with my first three steps."

He nodded.

The stands had grown silent. Most of the team was in the front row, with more guys lined up along the chain-link fence. I recognized Brady, leaning close against the chains, and Tommy beside him, looking anxious. Tony Gilmore, Brian Freeman, and several other players were kneeling by the fence. Standing a little away from the others was our safety, long, tall Ed Bent. He had his work cut out for him, seeing as how he was also center on our basketball team and his seasons overlapped. Looking through all the players who were either lined up along the fence or sitting in the front row, I somehow found Sam in the center of the third row. She grinned down at me with two thumbs up. Just the sight of her gave me a boost.

Then just behind her I saw an angry face, one that stood out from all the rest. It belonged to Matt Burris, who technically shouldn't even have been there. He was still suspended, but who was going to rat out Cam's best friend?

I felt myself crumbling. Matt was so good, much better than I'd ever be.

The coach blew a short blast on his whistle. I took a

deep breath, forced myself to look away from the crowd, and trotted over toward Cam.

"Okay, guys," Coach said. "Let's throw the ball around. Cam, don't get ahead of yourself. Start off slow. Keep it easy. Give him something he can catch without running. Just warm up."

Cam and I both walked to midfield and he flipped me an easy one. It sure didn't take the Great Receiver to catch that one.

I put out both hands and caught two fistfuls of air.

To me, it sounded like the entire stands erupted into laughter. Most of the guys at the chain-link fence collapsed against the chains and went into hysterics.

Cam couldn't control himself. He was laughing so hard he had both arms across his chest trying to hold it in.

Neither of the coaches was amused.

Coach Miller marched over to Cam. Whatever he said wiped the smile off Cam's lips and he faced me with only a trace of a smirk, ready to throw again.

Okay, Joey, I told myself firmly. You got the nerves out now. Think of the mechanics. Stop thinking of Matt up there. Stop thinking of anything except catching the ball.

Cam loped back a few feet, turned and threw a long ball. It came right at me in a classic spiral. I stumbled, reached toward the sky, missed the ball, and took a pratfall.

The stands went insane.

My face was hotter than a soldering iron. I could imagine my expression as Cam threw again and I missed that one, too. I thought of Sam back there, suffering along with me. She'd be whispering encouragement to me and trying hard not to close her eyes for the next catch. Mary Pat was somewhere up there, too. I imagined what she must be saying to Logan right about now.

And finally managed to catch a ball.

The stands moaned in disappointment at my having spoiled my perfect record, but Coach nodded at me and yelled, *"That's better, Eastland! Keep your focus! One thing at a time! Basics!"*

My heart was thundering, but I nodded back.

Cam's next ball flew off my fingertips, but I caught the two after that. The crowd settled down, watching again.

The coach motioned us to put some distance between us. Then Cam started throwing hard bee-bees, straight and fast.

Ping, ping, ping.

Let's see you catch this one. And this one. Cam threw harder. Faster.

Within a couple of minutes, the ball was coming at me so hard you'd think he was trying to break both my hands. But something inside of me had kicked into gear. The GR himself seemed to have moved into my body. I felt him inside me, alert and ready, flexing his muscles. Nothing gets past me, I thought. Nothing.

Cam's face was grim. He threw harder yet. The balls came at me like bullets from all angles. One high; the next knee-height. A foot either side of me, making me lunge sideways to make the catch.

"McKey!" Coach bellowed. He waved us both over.

Coach Stanley gave me a grinning thumbs-up, but there wasn't even a hint of a smile on Coach Miller's lips.

"You think I'm an idiot?" he said in Cam's face. "Is that what you think? That I don't know what you're doing?"

Cam's face was red. "What am I doing?"

"It's called sabotage," the coach said. "Keep it up and I won't just be looking for a new receiver, I'll be looking for a new quarterback. Your job is to connect with your receiver. We've already got plenty of players who can drop your passes. I have no idea how Joey's holding onto them, but you're making him look real good."

"Good?" Cam repeated disbelievingly. "Did you see how he started out?"

"I'm interested in end results," the coach snapped. "I could care less if he started out missing three out of four soap bubbles blown by a child of two."

"Coach, he's after somebody else's position!"

"He's after a *vacant* position," the coach said savagely. "Do what I tell you!"

After that Cam started throwing regulation passes. Pretty soon we were an unlikely team.

Blood roared in my ears, and I could hardly hear the coach calling out instructions. "Joey, give me a deep post. I want to see a throw, catch, and run in stride. Try to get to the twenty by the count of five! Get ready—*go!*"

It was the longest pass we'd tried, more than forty yards. A lot of high school quarterbacks couldn't even throw that far, but all it took from Cam was a flick of his wrist. I streaked downfield, looked over my shoulder, and there it was, coming straight at me. I reached out and tried not to think about dropping it. Two hands, I thought.

Here we go, bud! Piece of cake! It was *him* talking to me. The Great Receiver.

I nailed the catch and kept going, straight into the end zone.

Touchdown!

"Nice one!" Coach Miller yelled. "Let's try it again!"

Cam's face was a blur now. It was his hands that I watched. The slant of his body. The direction of his head as he looked one way and threw another. I forgot it was Cam out there throwing. I forgot it was me catching.

Soon Coach Stanley was working with me, making adjustments. "Good job, but learn to make those cuts crisper." "Make sure that an eight-yard out is eight yards, not six yards or seven." "Catch the ball before you run with it."

An hour passed as if it were five minutes. When the whistle blew, Cam and I walked toward the coaches. Coach Stanley was waiting for me with a high five.

I couldn't believe what I'd just done, and from the incredulous look on Cam's face I could see he believed it even less. Sweat poured off me. Cam was just as soaked. He wasn't looking at me. His mouth was clenched and he didn't look pleased to have just completed a high percentage of passes.

"That was a good beginning," Coach Miller said. "With some work, I think you two can make a great team."

Cam said absolutely nothing. He just stood there with the ball under his arm. Then, through a tight jaw, he finally said what was on his mind. "Forget it. I don't hang out with losers and I don't throw to them. You want me off the team, kick me off."

The warm breeze had died. The trees were still. White clouds stood motionless in the sky. Everything was quiet, even Cam's friends by the fence.

Suddenly, clear as a gong, I heard Tony Gilmore's high tenor voice proclaiming for everyone to hear: "Joey's got the real stuff! Nobody can say any different!"

I dared a glance at Matt Burris, who looked ready to kill somebody. Namely, me.

Coach Miller turned to Cam. "Calm down, young man. Let me make one thing clear. I'm in charge here. If I wanted you off this team, you'd be off in a heartbeat. But I don't want you off. You're a damn good quarterback, and you're the leader of this team. You're also smart enough to know that Joey can help us win. My decision is not up for discussion. He's going in."

Cam looked toward the fence and then back at me. He took a deep breath, held it, and then let it go. Finally he said, "You're the coach. But I still think Matt got robbed. And that's all I have to say." He took off his backward baseball cap, wiped the sweat off of his face with his arm, and left the field without another word.

Coach Miller put his hand on my shoulder. He looked at Cam walking toward Matt, who had left the bleachers and gone to meet him. "It's not you, son. There's a lot more going on with Cam than you realize. He and Matt are best friends. In the meantime, enjoy this moment. You just made starting wide receiver for the Bulldogs, and that's some accomplishment." He laughed, grabbed a form out of his shorts' pocket, and handed it to me. "Here's your permission form. Be sure you get it signed and bring it to practice tomorrow, okay?"

"Sure. Thanks, Coach."

All of a sudden it was over. The coaches were heading back up the hill to the office, and I was by myself on the field. Most of the team had left. I saw Ed Bent leaving for the parking lot, Melvin Barr behind him. Cam, Matt, the Doogan brothers, and Brian Freeman were already up there, standing on the sidewalk and talking with some of the others. None of the team had come over to offer congratulations. Instead they had almost seemed disappointed.

But there was scattered applause from the rest of the stands. I caught a glimpse of Perry Toomey looking satisfied as he skipped down the steps, probably thinking that if I wasn't much of a lab partner, at least I had added another kind of status to our lopsided combo. Plus I had avenged him with Matt.

Sam came running toward me with a glowing face. Logan and Mary Pat were close behind.

"You were wonderful, Joey." Sam grinned.

"My, yes," Mary Pat agreed enthusiastically. "I did think you would never get started though, didn't you, Logan?"

Logan shook my hand. "I thought you did really great, Joey. Honest."

They all had to leave. Logan was late to band practice, Mary Pat had to go get her hair cut, and Sam's mother was waiting in the parking lot to take her to babysit her cousin. In minutes, I found myself standing alone in an almost deserted stadium. Even with Sam, Mary Pat, and Logan's congratulations, it all seemed a little flat without somebody from the team saying something to me.

Face it, I told myself. They wanted Matt. They don't

want you. And by the way, you're still no closer to the loop than you ever were.

I went to the locker room for my stuff and started walking toward the parking lot, where my bike was chained. A few cars still dotted the lot, but there was only one other person at the bicycle rack. It was Tony. He was straddling his own bike, waiting for me.

Shocked, I realized he had put up his hand for a high five. Until I had been his water boy, I'd hardly known him except for being one of his fans. I took all accelerated classes; he was a level down, which meant we didn't share classes. He had always treated me well, saying thanks or smiling when I gave him a towel, water, or a cup for Gatorade. Being the team's star running back, I assumed he was in the loop. He was a decent kid.

"Congrats, Receiver," he said as we slapped hands. "Great tryout. I heard you made the team."

"You heard what the coach said?"

"Nah. Cam told everybody you made it. I knew it anyhow, after that tryout."

"Thanks for saying what you did out there."

"I wasn't lying. You do have the real stuff."

I grinned. "I guess Matt was thrilled?"

"Sure." He laughed. "He and Cam were both dancin' in the street. You want to ride home together? You're just a couple of blocks from my place. I live in those apartments up the road from you."

"Great. How'd you know where I live?"

"I've been delivering your paper every morning for the last month. I traded routes. Let's get going."

We took off pedaling. I noticed that neither of our bikes was new or top of the line.

"Where did you learn to catch a ball like that?" he asked.

"Hardware."

"Huh?"

"It's a long story."

I told him about it as we rode. Then we talked about everything from football to school to Tony's paper route.

"It helps my mom," he said. "She's on her own since Dad took off, and a secretary's salary doesn't go very far with four kids."

"I'm sorry about that, Tony. I didn't know. Your dad doesn't come to see you play?"

"Nah." He shrugged. "But Mom never misses a game. Say, your mom works at the Humane Society, doesn't she? I saw her in assembly last year after you got that grant money for the animals."

"Mrs. Cunningham helped get the grant through. I could never have done it alone."

"She's an impressive lady. Listen, I've been thinking of adopting a dog. I wouldn't mind having that Bulldog mascot. I heard he's over there."

My heart lurched, but I knew I shouldn't pass up a good home for Max.

"You say you have three brothers and sisters?"

"Make that three sisters," he said, laughing. "I'm the only man in the house now." Saying that, his smile disappeared and he looked away, studying the trees we were passing.

"About Max," I said after a few minutes of silent biking.

"That his name?"

"Yeah. Are your sisters older than you or younger?"

"Younger. Ninth, sixth, and fourth grades. Why?"

"Are they good with animals?"

"Oh, yeah! We've always had a dog. We lost Tiki Barber last year," he said dejectedly. "He was pretty old when we got him from the pound, but we fell in love with him."

"Wonder how he got his name."

He laughed a little. "Yeah. Good old Tiki. I thought I might name my new dog LT for LaDainian Tomlinson, but I guess he already has a name."

I nodded, pained at the thought of Max's losing his name even if his new one belonged to a great football player. "Yep."

"So, is he available?"

"Well, right now, he's mine, but . . ." I hesitated, trying to like the idea of giving him to Tony. What kind of a selfish pig was I to want to hang on to him when he had a chance for a good permanent home? But my heart froze at the idea.

"After the season ends, I might have to let him go," I finally said reluctantly. "So if you're interested . . ."

"If he's yours," Tony said, "keep him. Dogs know who their humans are, just like humans know who their dogs are. I want to find my own dog, not steal yours. Maybe I'll go to the Society next weekend to look."

"There are some great dogs there. You'll find one for sure."

"Bet you can't wait to tell your folks what happened in your tryout."

"They don't even know about it. Dad will be happy. But my mom? Let's just say you should wish me luck getting my form signed. She'd rather have me sign up to blast underwater caves or go skydiving."

"C'mon. She'll be thrilled."

"I hope. But she, well, she's got a kind of condition."

He looked at me cautiously. "You mean she's sick?"

"Not that kind of sick. It's just that she always expects the absolute worse to happen. She might not let me play."

"Think positive, Joey."

"Okay." I drew a deep breath. "She's going to let me play and she's going to love it. She'll be so anxious to sign the form, she'll probably rip it right out of my hand!"

Tony grinned. "Perfect!" he said.

13

"Not in a thousand years," Mom said, when I put the form in her hand. The form accepted parental responsibility for all sorts of injuries, including death. She shook her head sadly. "Honey, please understand. I'd be a basket case. I'd be worrying every minute. No, every second. It's . . . it's just . . . impossible."

"But you let me do tryouts."

"I must have been out of my mind," she said, white-faced. "But looking at this form . . . I just can't sign it. I'm sorry." She was almost crying.

She had turned off most of the living room lights, and it was unusually quiet. The snakes, lost again only this morning, had been found in P.S.'s bed where he'd hidden them overnight; now they were back in their tank. The cats had been banished from the room for the day after hanging around the tank too much. Astro and Echo were in the backyard. Only Max was on the couch with us, his head on Mom's lap. Her hand trembled as she reached to scratch behind his ears.

"You know I'm in your corner, honey," Mom said miserably. "There isn't anything I wouldn't do for you. But you know our luck. You'd be the one who got hurt. I just know it!"

"Mom, I know you worry a lot. But you're not really telling me our family is jinxed?" I stared at her. "Come on, Mom."

She had her "something terrible is coming our way" look. Her chin was trembling. "Not jinxed; I didn't mean *that*." She cleared her throat, then went on in a choked voice. "It's just that, you know, things happen to us. Like Logan's test. And me losing my wallet in the grocery."

"Lots of kids mess up on their SATs, Mom. And lots of people lose their wallets."

"With four hundred dollars cash inside?"

"Ah . . ." I tried to think. "To be honest, I don't think I ever knew anyone whose wallet *had* four hundred in cash inside it. Mom, please."

"It wasn't *my* money," she continued doggedly. "It was PTA money. And I had to replace it. And what about the snakes always getting out and scaring people?"

"We have a houseful of animals, and it's our fault that the lid to the snake tank is so easy to open. P.S. has been opening that tank since he learned how to walk. One of these days, one of the cats is going to open it. And it's not like we don't have good latches available. Dad owns a hardware store!" I sighed. "Mom, this is about football, not jinxes. It's about me doing something I'm dying to do."

"It's about broken bones, Joey." She shuddered. "Concussions. Even worse."

Max whimpered and crawled from Mom's lap to mine.

Then he looked back at Mom, trying to figure out which of us was in worse shape.

"Mom . . ."

She shook her head and handed the form back to me. "I *can't*. Please, Joey. Don't ask me."

After a long moment, I said hoarsely, "Okay." Now it was me who was shaking. I picked up Max and left Mom sitting alone in the almost dark room. It was over. I'd had my tryout, somehow aced it, and still I couldn't play.

Slowly, I sank into my desk chair, still holding Max and lacking even the strength to climb up to my bunk. It was getting late; everything outside the window was fading into a dark blur. After a while I heard Mom in the kitchen. Usually I set the table. But I couldn't move, not even when I heard doors slamming downstairs and people talking and knew that Dad and Logan had come home for dinner.

Mom came to the foot of the stairs and called, "Dinner's ready, honey! Come down now!"

I sat silently, my throat too tight to answer. Max hovered against my chest, his head turned up to mine, his tongue making mournful sweeps across my face. "It'll be all right, boy," I whispered. I wasn't sure which one of us I was lying to.

Downstairs, I heard talking: Dad's puzzled voice and Logan's angry one and under them both, Mom's weeping. Then just the clatter of plates as they got on with an almost silent dinner.

Almost an hour later, Dad knocked on my door and stuck his head in. "Okay if I come in? I brought you an emergency snack."

I looked at the loaded plate of chicken, stuffing and gravy, peas, and buttered bread. "Some snack," I said, trying to smile. "But I'm not hungry."

He dragged over Logan's desk chair, set the plate on my desk, and took a seat. I picked up a piece of bread, took a bite, and put it back down.

Dad ran nervous fingers through what was left of his hair. "I've been doing some thinking. Let's talk."

"What's the use? She won't give in."

"Well, you know how she is. She worries. All mothers worry about their kids. Even when they're teenagers." He cleared his throat, not looking at me.

"Not like her," I mumbled, petting Max's head. "The other guys' moms let them play."

He sighed, then smiled. "Logan said you had a great tryout today. I wish you'd told me. I'd have been there," he added.

"I would have invited you if I'd known it would be good. If it was awful, I didn't want you there."

"Right. In any case, I'm glad it went so well." He sat still on Logan's chair for a few seconds, then abruptly stood up like he'd just made a decision. He pointed down at the crumpled piece of paper on my desk. "Is that it?"

I nodded.

Without another word, he smoothed it out and looked at it. Then he picked up a pen and scribbled his name. "You're cleared."

The paper blurred in front of my eyes. "You signed it? But you *never* disagree with each other. If one of you says no, that's it."

"I know. But Mom doesn't quite understand how much you want this. I do, because I was out there throwing all those balls to you. And watching you and Logan stock shelves," he added, grinning. "If I made a decision based on something your mom knew more about than me, I would expect her to . . ." He cleared his throat.

"Override you?"

"Yeah, I would. Your mom's got it rough. Working all day at the Society, taking care of you kids and the animals, cooking, cleaning, you name it. She's too tired to notice you going out at all hours to run. She doesn't realize how you felt not making the team. Anyway just because Mom worries too much, it doesn't mean we have to. Aren't you getting tired of living like you're afraid of everything?"

"Yeah, a little."

"Me too," he admitted, scratching that same sparse place on his scalp. There were circles under his eyes, and his body, already on the scrawny side, looked like he'd lost some weight from the long hours he worked and the constant worry about money.

I thought about all those hours we'd shared in the park and how much we'd both enjoyed them. He hadn't been a jock in school, had never played anything except a little tennis and golf, but he was a couch warrior on weekends, watching the pros play. On Sundays, he, Logan and I watched sports together hour after hour, each of us setting up fantasy teams, talking strategy, and rooting our teams on. I wouldn't have traded those times for millions in the bank. Lately even P.S. had been in the thick of it, gobbling chips and cheering with the rest of us.

"Dad?"

"Yes?"

"I heard Logan downstairs. What was he saying?"

Dad grinned. "Your brother said that Mary Pat's family has an old dusty room over their garage. He threatened to ask them if he could move into it if Mom didn't let you play."

I smiled. Say what you would about Logan, he was a true brother.

Dad looked at Max, who still sat patiently on my lap with his tail wagging. "Hope he brings you some luck this season." He clapped his hand to my shoulder and headed for the door, leaving me wondering if I'd dreamed the entire thing. I picked up the slip and looked at his signature on the parental permission line: William Eastland.

It was happening! I was going to play on the team!

Staring through the dark window, absently chewing on cold chicken, I imagined myself walking into school after one of our games, where I'd caught everything Cam had thrown and we'd beaten a really good team. The first thing I'd hear coming into the lobby would be Cam's voice. He'd yell, "Hey, Joey! Over here!"

Everyone would see me walk over to the loop. See the A-list pound me on the back. Cute girls would take notice. At last I would be somebody.

14

The next morning Mom's eyes were red.

"Hurry up and eat," she said, putting cereal and toast on the table. "We need to leave. I overslept." She looked more like she hadn't slept at all. As for me, I'd tossed and turned and ended up oversleeping, too. It was too late to bike to school.

I slipped into my chair and looked up at her. "Did . . . did you talk to Dad?"

She pretended she hadn't heard me, looking out the window and saying with false brightness, "Looks like a nice day."

I swallowed my breakfast in large gulps and ran for my books. I jumped into the car next to P.S., who started crumbling his muffin and throwing the crumbs at me. She still hadn't mentioned the permission slip.

"Mom? Is everything okay?"

"Fine," she said stiffly. "P.S., stop making a mess back there." She drove in silence through the streets and behind the sparser-than-usual line of cars at school, all late arrivals, and waited for me to leave the car.

I climbed out and looked at her uncertainly through the window. "Have a good day, Mom."

She finally looked at me, summoning a somewhat ragged smile. "Just take care, okay?"

"I will, Mom. I promise." I watched her drive slowly away and knew it would be hard for her. But maybe in the end she'd learn to worry less.

"Watch out, Eastland," Cam said as I walked through the lobby door to find the warning bell dinging. "Your best bud looks to have a dead rat on top of his head. Hey, Tombstone, does your mom cut your hair?"

He strolled down the hall, followed by several of his gang, mostly other team members, all laughing snidely and looking toward the door.

I looked back to see Perry Toomey hurrying in, loaded down with a stack of books and an overflowing backpack. Cam turned back around, pointing at Perry's head.

"Was it a pet, Toomey, or a relative?"

"Cram it up your entoprocta!" Perry shot back, sticking his chest out. His brown hair did kind of sprawl on his scalp like something dead.

"What's that?" Cam muttered, his eyes narrowing.

"You don't want to know," Perry replied.

"And you want me to cram something up there? How will you make me do that? Oooh, I'm so scared of those power fists of yours." Cam pretended to shudder.

Perry pretended to shudder right back. "And I'm terrified of that power brain of yours. I heard you finally learned your alphabet."

Cam moved on, saying over his shoulder, "Don't let Tombstone's mom near your hair, Eastland."

Perry sneered and scampered on toward the stairs, intent on getting to class before the last bell.

"Hey, Joey." Tony came up beside me, wearing a backpack and carrying an armload of books. A canvas bag weighted down one shoulder. A girl ran behind him carrying a small case.

"That's Peggy, my sister," he said, jerking his head back at her.

"Hi," Peggy panted, struggling to keep up.

"Hey." I noticed she was a beauty.

Tony shifted the canvas bag to his other shoulder. It slumped immediately.

"What's in there?" I asked. "Rocks?"

He grimaced. "Matter of fact, yeah."

"What?" I took a look into the bag. Sure enough, it was crammed with rocks of all sizes and shapes.

"They're for Peggy's science class," he explained. "Hurry up, Peg! Put your flute in the band room. I'll carry your rocks upstairs and leave them in your science room."

"Thanks!" She flew toward the band room with the case.

"Your sister's gorgeous, Tony," I said, trying not to gawk.

"Tell me about it," he said. "The phone never stops ringing, but she only dates Mom's best friend's son, if you want to call trips to the movies, driven by a parent, or family outings to the beach dating." He glanced at the hall clock as we trudged upstairs. "I can't believe we got here on time. Mom's old car died two blocks from school. A cop stopped to help her, and Peg and I took off running. Hang on a sec." He ducked into a room and came out without the rocks. "Whew. You get your form signed okay?"

I nodded and said uneasily, "I hope Cam's not on my case on the field like he is here at school, or there'll be trouble."

"He won't be," Tony said. "Not if he wants to look good himself. And believe me, he wants to look *real* good out there. He wants to be a pro quarterback, you know."

My eyebrows went up. "No, I didn't. You think he has a shot?"

Tony shrugged. "Who knows? I used to think about being a pro. Then one day I looked in the mirror and saw this scrawny little body. And I thought, It ain't gonna happen."

"You're pretty amazing out there."

He shrugged. "I'm okay for high school, but I wasn't built to go any further."

"I'm sorry," I mumbled.

"Naw, don't be. I'll go to college and be something else. Maybe an architect. I like to draw things to scale and then make them. Now *you* could have that dream, maybe. If you really wanted to, that is."

"Being an architect? I was thinking more of going into law."

He grinned. "I meant playing pro ball. You've got a great stride. Good receiver body."

My brain went numb. A pro? Was he seriously talking about my being a professional wide receiver?

We headed to separate homerooms. As I dropped into the desk next to Sam's, the last bell rang. Before I could say anything, Ashley Parker looked over and said, "Hey, Joey."

"Hey." I wondered if my chick farm remark had struck her as cooler than it had Nancy Frazier. Maybe she was finally warming up to me. She *had* winked, after all.

"I was walking by the field on my way to cheerleading yesterday," she murmured, fluffing her blond hair. "I saw part of your tryout. Pretty awesome."

"Thanks," I said, trying to play it cool.

"You're just soooo awesome, Joey," Sam muttered beside me, fluttering her eyelashes as Nancy and Ashley started whispering. "Isn't it weird how I thought you were garbage yesterday morning, but then yesterday afternoon I noticed you could catch a football and now I think you're a total cutie?"

"It wasn't Ashley who treated me like that," I reminded her. "It was Nancy."

"Oh, yeah, Ashley is the sensitive type. I forgot."

"Knock it off, Sam," I hissed, as Mr. Anderson, our homeroom teacher, frowned in our direction.

"I'll knock it off," she whispered back, "when you stop drooling over Miss Airhead. Come on, Joey, she thinks the answer to world peace is a good hairdo."

"I said to drop it." I was ticked at her for trying to ruin my fantasies. After all Ashley had gone out of her way to speak to me a couple of times. Like when I fell over the curb. I should have realized at the time she was laughing *with* me, not *at* me.

Of course I had to make allowances for Sam. She

wasn't used to girls flirting with me. And it was true that Ashley hadn't seemed to notice me much before my tryout.

But maybe she really loved how you looked out there, I thought. What's wrong with being suddenly discovered? She saw a different you out there on the field, and she liked what she saw. Didn't I always say she had mystery and insight?

"She's not who you imagine she is," Sam whispered. "Remember what I'm telling you, Joey. It may save you a bad time."

But I was looking sideways at Ashley who was sitting on one leg in her seat, twisting the chain around her neck, her blond hair curling softly against her cheek. She saw me looking and smiled slowly back.

15

That afternoon I lived a dream. I was given a locker, a play-book, and a practice uniform. I taped a picture of Max to the inside of my locker door, stuffed my backpack, books, and school clothes inside, and stood there, an official Bull-dog right down to the helmet swinging from my fingers.

I poked at my padding uneasily, feeling as awkward as if someone had just tied a bale of cotton around my shoulders. I was also padded at the knees, thighs, hips, and tailbone. Even though my pads were lighter than the linemen's, I still had that stuffed turkey feeling.

From all sides teammates watched me tug at my shoulders and adjust my pants. So far Tony had been the only one to start a conversation—with the exception of a few mutters from players such as Ricardo Gonzalez, Ed Bent, and Melvin Barr. Maybe that was because Cam was one of the first dressed and stood with his arms folded across his chest, moodily staring across the locker room, daring anyone to welcome me to the team.

"Here you are, Joey!" a friendly voice said behind me.

The rock in my stomach dissolved a little as I turned

around to find Karen Harris standing there. "Oh, Karen, I'm sorry. I forgot to tell you and the rest of the crew."

Karen grinned wryly. "I think we all got the news. We'll be okay, though I won't say you won't be missed. You were a terrific jack-of-all-trades. But I'm happy for you. Besides, we're still on the same team!" She put out a hand and shook mine warmly. "Good luck!"

The practice was about to start when Tony ran in. "Peg lost her flute and she went nuts," he panted, hurrying to change clothes. "It turned up in the office. She'd left it in the hall after band. I've chased that flute all over school, home, and points past."

We walked out together to find a good number of people in the bleachers. Apparently a lot of people wanted to take a look at the hydration-therapist-turned-into-a-wide-receiver. The cheerleaders were on the sidelines, keeping an eye on the field between their exercises. I saw a slim blonde in shorts waving at me, and my stomach lurched. My hand stole up a little, only to fall as Nancy quickly pulled Ashley away.

Halfway through our conditioning drills we put the helmets on, just as I was breathing a sigh of relief at finding the pads no real problem. But the second my helmet was on, I felt trapped, as though I had just stuck my head in a cage. It was a hot day. Sweat rolled down. I could hardly turn my head.

"My helmet's too big, Tony. It slid a little when I looked up."

"So let it."

"How am I going to see the ball if my helmet is sliding?"

"Turn your head." He watched carefully as I looked from left to right and then up. "It fits. Trust it."

I tried it again and finally nodded. "Okay. I think I can get used to it. After maybe two years."

He grinned. "C'mon. You'll be okay."

"Yeah." But at the moment I couldn't have zeroed in on an elephant, much less a football.

Coach Miller blew his whistle and aimed a straight arm at the far side of the field. "Defense with Coach Brewster over there!" Coach Brewster was the third coach for the team when he wasn't coaching soccer. In the spring he coached JV baseball. In his spare time he taught geometry.

Pretty soon I found myself in midfield with Coach Miller and Coach Stanley. Cam and George White, the center, were there, too, along with our offensive line, runners, and two tight ends. The two burly guards were Roddy Doogan and José Lopez; the two tacklers, Ambrose Morse and Jackson Allen, were both huge muscle machines. Wayne Yeager was the other wide receiver. The tight ends, Brian Freeman and Andy Doogan, would come in and out as the plays dictated. Tony was our halfback, and Melvin Barr was our tougher-than-nails fullback. There were also a handful of reserves.

I took a deep breath to savor the moment. I was finally here.

Coach Miller looked my way. "Eastland, you're going to have to learn that playbook as quickly as possible. You understand the basic I formation?"

Red-faced, I saw the others looking at me and nodded. "I know the basics. I'll juice up on anything else. I know I'm playing catch-up."

"You'll get there. Line up wide right."

It was my first formation ever, except in park flag. From all directions, eyes bored holes in me. Nothing was going to come free. I was the new kid on the block, and I'd have to prove myself.

Wayne was wide left, on the opposite side of the field, and he was one of the unhappiest at my being there. His hopes of turning into the key receiver were fading fast, especially since the coach was saving his twisted ankle by having me run all the receiver plays while he merely lined up.

I looked toward the stands and, sure enough, there was Matt Burris hunkered down on the second row of the bleachers, watching the twerp who had taken his position. *Yesterday,* he was telling me with his cold eyes, *was an accident. Show me again if you're such a great receiver.*

Tommy Brink was also on the sidelines. He was out of the receiver spot, back to being second-string running back, and his nose looked as out of joint as Matt's. Ashley and the rest of the cheerleaders were watching, too.

If only, I thought, I could take my helmet off for just the first few plays.

Sweat streaked down my face, and I fought wanting to reach through the helmet and dry it. Right here, wearing this stupid contraption over my head, was where it could all end for me.

The coach's whistle blew, and Cam yelled, "Hut! Hut! Hut!"

I was shaking so much I could hardly stand up, much less run.

"*Ho!*" Coach yelled, killing the play.

Maybe he'd seen through my facemask and had found a ghost looking back at him. "Give me two laps first," he yelled. "All except Wayne."

Back to his old tricks, I thought. Running off the nerves.

The offense all headed for the track with their helmets off. I reached up to take mine off, and there came another whistle.

"Eastland! Leave yours on!"

I knew that to keep up with Tony, I'd have my work cut out for me, especially hampered with a helmet. But I meant to try. At the whistle, I shot forward. As always, the first few steps were not my strength. As I'd expected Tony streaked ahead of me, with Brian Freeman and Cam not far behind him. I came next, with George White and Andy Doogan. Melvin Barr thudded behind us, being built for the short, tough run, not for speed. The guards and tackles ran behind us all, powerhouses on the move, bruising space as they thundered through it.

Pick up your knees, Receiver! I ordered myself. Your kneecaps aren't wearing helmets. Go-go-go!

I picked up speed and saw Cam's sweat-streaked face glaring at me as I passed him. Midway into the first lap, I was ahead of everyone except Brian and Tony. Pumping harder, I pounded by Brian and saw him look up in surprise.

"Hey, Receiver," Tony grunted. The two of us were in a neck-and-neck race, with a lap to go.

"Hey!"

We ran without another word, each using the other to gain more speed, flying into the second lap shoulder to shoulder. That's when I pulled ahead. His shorter legs might fly, but they could not keep up with my long stride. I finished all alone, Tony about twenty yards back. He trotted over to me with a grin, and we watched the others finish up behind us.

By the time we lined up again, my nervous attack had dissolved. The first ball Cam threw was over my head and out in front of me by a foot. I accelerated into second gear and nailed it.

The cheerleaders were cheering when I trotted back with the ball. Cam looked like I'd just thrown a mud cake at him. "That pass wasn't that hard to catch," he said. "That stupid showboating makes me look bad. Lay off!"

Brian Freeman looked at me with the same appraising look he had used when I passed him on the track. He waited until Cam huffed off and muttered, "All the same, not bad, Eastland. Not bad at all."

The next play, I ran the wrong direction and collided with Melvin Barr, ending up on my butt.

"We're on the same team, in case you didn't notice," Melvin huffed, but he stuck out a hand to pull me up.

After that I forgot about the helmet on my head, the sweat running down my face, and the people watching. I dropped some balls, but caught more than I dropped.

"Key on the ball, Eastland! Follow the ball into your hands. Catch it, cut, and run! Be precise!"

I learned to run a crisp route. My hands became glue.

Everything that Cam threw ended up stuck to them. In the distance I heard people cheering from the bleachers.

Coach Stanley yelled, "Nice catch, Eastland! Next time explode off that pivot! Better!"

Coach Miller gave out no compliments at all. He just watched and made adjustments.

I stopped worrying about mistakes. Nothing mattered but that I was out there at last.

After a while Coach Miller brought in the defense and we practiced patterns, play action passes, and handoffs. We did shuffle passes and quarterback sneaks. Coach also threw in a couple of deep post patterns. I ran the wrong way the first time, but picked up the second. Not perfect, but not bad.

"Good enough," Tony said, running by me to line up.

"We're getting there," the coach said. "This is working, guys. We're turning into a triple-threat team. We've got passing, running, and defense."

When we were finished, there were a few muttered words of "way to go" in my direction, mainly from Brian and Melvin. But mostly the team kept quiet. Cam headed toward the bleachers where Matt was waiting, and Brady and George followed, along with Brian, Tommy, Wayne, and several other players.

I stared after them. I might be on the team, but I was a long way away from being one of them.

"Take it off," Tony said suddenly, snapping me out of my thoughts.

"Huh? Take what off?" I asked.

"Your helmet. Practice is over."

I hadn't even realized I still had it on. I unsnapped it and took it off, then dried my face with the sleeve of my jersey. My hair was dripping. I jerked my head at Cam and his friends. Most were now straggling toward the locker room. Cam and Matt kept talking, heads together.

"Do they hate me for taking Matt's place? Is that it?"

"Not all that many people like to see others succeed," Tony said.

"They like to see *you* when you run touchdowns."

"I told you. I'm not a threat. I don't have a future in sports, and they know it. With you, it could be different."

I glanced toward the bleachers and saw Ashley staring my way. She waved, and I waved back, probably with a sappy grin on my face. A second later I saw Sam walking down the bleacher steps, heading for the gate. She was staring at me, too. Or actually, more like glaring.

Tony looked after Sam. He started to say something, then let it ride. Instead he looked back at Cam and Matt Burris, who were still huddled together. Matt's head shook furiously. Cam put a hand on his shoulder as if to calm him down and kept talking. Matt stopped interrupting and listened. Finally he nodded.

"What are they up to?" Tony muttered. "I don't like it."

"There's nothing they can do," I said. "I have the spot."

"Just watch your back."

"You don't think they'd really . . .?"

"I doubt it, knowing that Cam could get kicked off the team along with Matt. But those two are crazy enough to take chances. Just . . . heads up, okay?"

"Yeah, sure." Uneasily, I noticed they had turned and were staring right at me.

"How come you're willing to hang out with me?" I asked him. "Aren't you afraid it'll hurt your popularity?"

He laughed. "What popularity? With Cam? He doesn't know me from crabgrass."

"You're kidding," I said slowly. But come to think of it, I had never really noticed Tony in the loop. I had only assumed he must be there. "You're the star halfback. The best runner on the team."

"That and a bus token might get me a few blocks. Frankly, Joey, I could care less."

As we walked toward the locker room, I realized I envied him even more than if he had been in the loop. I envied him that he didn't care.

16

"You'll be the first athlete our family ever produced," Grandpa Bobby said at dinner Wednesday night.

I looked queasily at the congealed salad Grandma Heidi had brought and then studied Mom's turkey loaf. Grandma Edith, Dad's mother, had brought a squash casserole. I was glad I'd let Tony talk me into a double-chocolate milkshake after my second—and better—practice.

"I think I had an aunt that used to row a canoe," Grandma Heidi mused. "At camp or something."

"Your daddy could swim," Grandma Edith said to Dad, her eyes misting. We'd lost Grandpa Howie to pneumonia last year. "I can float."

"I play a little golf when I can find time," Dad put in.

"I can walk from one room to another, so does that make me an athlete?" Grandpa Bobby asked. "Can't I compliment my own grandson without everyone having something to say?"

"I'm glad you have one grandson to be proud of," Logan said. "Try never to mention me. You wouldn't know what the heck to say."

Our grandparents raced each other to answer that.

"Grades like yours?" Grandpa said.

"Going to be a veterinarian?" Grandma Heidi said.

"Saxophone player?" Grandma Edith said.

Logan shot us all a look over the "Reason and Logic" book that Mary Pat had assigned him to study from cover to cover. Doing all the problems would take months, he had told me, but he didn't have months. His next SAT was less than three weeks away, so he carried the book and a pad and pen around with him everywhere he went.

Everywhere included the dinner table.

"I'm the last seat saxophonist in the worst marching high school band that ever stunk up a football field," Logan said. "And forget vet school. Face it, I'm a loser."

"Never call yourself that," Mom said, white-faced. She had been practically silent over dinner. Since Dad had signed my form, she hadn't been herself.

Dad looked up at her, and she immediately looked away. "Mom's right, son," he mumbled, staring back down at his plate. "You're practically a straight-A student."

"I'm still a loser," Logan insisted. "The one who comes in last in every race."

The table fell silent. I felt the hollowness in my brother's eyes clear down to my stomach. I knew that feeling, but I couldn't think of anything to say.

Neither could anyone else. Every face was set in worry and sadness.

"*Not* a loser," P.S. said suddenly around a mouthful of turkey loaf. He was the only one making much headway with it. Put ketchup on something and P.S. was a happy camper.

Logan looked at him. "I'm not?"

"You win when you race me."

"No, I don't," Logan reminded him. "You do."

P.S. stopped chewing. "You *let* me win," he said. "You're a winner, Logan!"

Max nudged my ankle under the table, and I slid him a piece of turkey loaf. With his bottomless pit of a stomach, I thought he'd scarf it up, but he spent several seconds licking it and even longer sniffing it. In the end, though, he gulped it down.

"Where did you get this idea about being a loser?" Dad asked Logan. "You think every smart person scores the perfect SAT the first time around? Look at Joey. Didn't he fail at two football tryouts and didn't he do better this time around?"

Logan said nothing, just went on nibbling at the scant amount of food he'd allowed himself, per Mary Pat's instructions.

"It's Mary Pat that's got him convinced he's a big nothing," I said. "She has all the answers, including how to get rid of love handles."

"Does she know how to get rid of a tummy?" Grandma Heidi asked, looking down at what she called her "spread."

"Portion control," I said. "Cut everything in half. You're allowed three tablespoons of cereal and enough milk to drown a fly. If it works for love handles, it'll work for everything else." I fed Max another piece of turkey loaf. It was growing on him. He gobbled it down in half a second and almost ate my fingers with it.

"Mary Pat," Logan said, busy working a logic problem

with his right hand and eating a dab of congealed salad with his left, "may not know everything, but she knows how to pass an SAT test. I'm doing it her way."

"The best thing for Mary Pat," Grandpa Bobby said thoughtfully, "might be to fail at something. Has she ever?"

"Nope," Logan said, "and I doubt she ever will. She's perfect in every way. Great at everything." His eyes glazed over.

"I don't know if you can be great at something if you haven't experienced being bad at something else," Grandpa Bobby said.

It had a nice ring to it, but Logan never looked up from his pad.

"Good to see so much study," Grandma Edith said encouragingly. "I'm sure it will pay off. It's wonderful to have two outstanding students in the family. P.S. will have a lot to live up to."

I kept my guilty eyes on my plate. In the last few days my studies had been the last thing on my mind. In fact I had done hardly anything. In accelerated classes "hardly anything" means big problems. Plus there was the international project hanging over me.

There was no help for it. I left the dinner table and went straight to my computer. Thanks to our grandparents, Logan and I each had one to ourselves. During the next couple of hours, time rolled back five thousand years. As hard as it was to believe, not one of the people I read about had even heard about the Lakewood Bulldogs football team.

17

The next morning our project team gathered at the front of the classroom and got our first glimpse of Kelsey Magnum and Ted Wyatt's artwork. In only three days they had begun a canvas, mingling their two styles.

Ted's animated tree creature, Stump, was transformed into watercolors. His trunk opened to throngs of people who danced together, some in couples, some in long, linked lines. Kelsey's watercolors flowered over and around the dancers, one image blooming into another.

"The people will be multicultured," Ted explained, pointing at a few drawings that had taken on definition. "All sizes, shapes, and colors."

"All celebrating understanding in the heart of the forest!" Kelsey added, so enthralled I hardly recognized her. She looked like a normal excited teenager. Her eyes shone.

"Outstanding beginning," Mrs. C. said, motioning us to our seats. "Now then. Samantha Burton, have you something to share with us on the topic of dominating cultures?"

Sam stared at the canvas. "Do we really need to write essays? The art says it much better, doesn't it?"

"Words can draw eloquent pictures, too. Besides, a lot

of the trouble in the world is caused by misusing words, so it seems fitting to use them to right some of the misunderstanding."

"Yes ma'am," Sam murmured. "I thought examples might be best to explain the difference between cultural exchange, assimilation, and domination." She didn't bother to glance at her notes. "For example, if American eye surgeons go into an African village and restore the sight of hundreds of people by removing cataracts, this is cultural exchange. If we help train their doctors, this is assimilation. But to bring them American clothing might change and, thereby, dominate their dress."

"Other examples?"

"Slavery, of course. Our slaves were often stolen from their native country."

Mrs. C. nodded. "Yes, and my people have had to pull ourselves up by the bootstraps to recover. Most of us have lost our ancestral African roots."

"Another example would be the way we treated Native Americans, taking their land, sticking them on barren reservations, and making them send their children to American boarding schools where they had to abandon their own religion and language."

"What might be an example of cultural exchange with our Native Americans, as opposed to domination?"

"We buy their art and recognize tribal sovereignty."

"Conclusions, Miss Burton?"

"We must be careful to interact with people from other cultures without trying to change them. If all countries had the same cultures, the world would lose a lot of its magic."

"I like what you say, Miss Burton!" Mrs. C. declared solemnly.

Perry Toomey plastered the blackboard with pictures of artifacts and went on and on about glass blowing, managing to make the historic progression of glass and ceramics duller than watching a cockroach inch across a door.

I slumped down in my seat, eyelids heavy as trunks. I was back on the field with the shrill sound of Cam yelling *Hut-hut-hut*, followed by the clanking of helmets butting into each other, the thud of players hitting the ground. The *umph* of players having their breath knocked out of them.

"*Here's* an interesting fact!" Perry's fist hit Mrs. C's desk enthusiastically, and I jumped in my seat, catching Sam's accusatory stare.

Perry's voice droned around my head like a bee looking for a hive. He was never going to stop. He would be here a hundred years from now, still talking, a white beard down to his knees.

Sam's elbow jabbed into my ribs, and my eyelids flew open.

Perry was back at his desk, and Mrs. C. was staring at me with a mixture of anger and disappointment that made me blush. I dove for my papers.

"Right," I mumbled, stumbling toward her desk, dropping pictures of chariots and horse racing along the way.

The project group seemed hostile about the equestrian facets of the ancient Olympics. I had an idea their anger had less to do with the Olympians and more to do with my sleeping in class. What did they expect after a restless night of imagining myself being carried on the shoulders of my team to the cheers of adoring fans?

I had no fans here.

Naturally I ended up at Mrs. C.'s desk after our meeting adjourned.

"You promised me, Eastland!"

"But I did the work! It took me hours! Look!" I showed her the printed pages, the notes.

"Where are *you* in all this, Eastland?" she asked, looking it over. "I see pages copied, pictures printed. Where are the thoughts *you* were to bring to us this morning? The beginnings of your own cultural understanding? Where is that?"

I was sorry to disappoint her, but why couldn't she understand that being on a football team was something I had dreamed about for as long as I could remember? I wanted space to enjoy it. For once, didn't I have the right to just have a good time? Mumbling an apology, I turned to leave the room.

Her voice stopped me at the door. "Incidentally, Eastland, who won the Olympics that first year?" As I stood gaping, trying to gather my thoughts, she went on. "Well then, who competed? Do you have the names? No? How about the second year? Who were those champions? Ah, just think, all those heroes forgotten."

She began to organize her desk for the coming day. I stood there for a moment wondering if she'd speak again, but she didn't look up.

* * *

My first class, French, was a temporary port in a storm since I'd had an excellent freshman year.

But biology was even worse than my Olympics fiasco. I had only skimmed the DNA lesson. Not only did I flounder in the class discussion when Mr. Adams called on me, but I also had to face a highly indignant Perry, who had already finished collecting his diverse DNA specimens, including cheek swabbings and a collection of test tubes filled with spit.

"I'm ready for gel electrophoresis," he said impatiently. "How can you dawdle like this when we're on the brink of separating DNA fragments and constructing fingerprints of the Lambda genome using diverse restriction enzymes? We should be setting up our schedule to go to Bioscope Systems."

"Perry, we have until next semester!"

"Well, of course, we should wait until the last second," he said sarcastically. "Why don't we see if Bioscope is open at midnight the night before the second term ends?" Sulking, he got on with the day's work of studying chromosomes under microscopes. At the end of class, he gathered his books and stormed past me without a backward glance.

In Honors Reading and Language Arts, Mrs. C. didn't look at me either. It felt terrible to be invisible to my favorite teacher. I tried to tell myself I didn't care, but the sick feeling in my gut continued through geometry, statistics, and U.S. history. I felt badly; I really did. I knew I was letting everyone down. A tiny voice reminded me I was letting myself down, too.

But came the afternoon practice and I forgot it all and went back to doing what I most wanted to do: running and catching footballs.

And when Tony said, "Let's go running tonight," I did not tell him that I had no time, that I was behind in my schoolwork. I nodded. "Okay."

"Great." He looked eager.

But for the first time in hours, I was not able to block the disturbing image of Perry's pale, pimpled face, his myopic eyes staring at me in disappointment. The memory sent a sickening, acidy flood rising from my stomach to my throat.

I'd get to biology later tonight, I promised myself. Or at least tomorrow.

Tony and I went jogging through the dark, our breath steaming, the familiar neighborhood lit only by our jacket reflectors, streetlights, and the houses we passed. Looking at Tony bounding beside me, his head barely clearing my shoulder, I felt fantastic.

"I like running in the dark," Tony declared. "I feel like I'm a spy or something. How'd you get started doing this?"

"I wanted to run when no one could see me."

He laughed. "Who's 'no one'?"

"People like Cam. I guess I'm afraid of what they think of me." I looked sideways at him, his shorter legs pumping harder than mine to cover the same space in the same time. "You've never been afraid of anything, have you?"

He didn't answer for a minute. In the shadowy haze of the streetlights, he looked much older.

"Actually I'm one of the most afraid people you'll ever meet," he said.

"No way. What do you have to be afraid of?"

He sighed. "For openers, that my dad will come home again. He came back three years ago for a while. He can be pretty tough."

"You mean . . . he didn't hit you or anything?"

"Didn't he? And he hit Mom, too. And slapped the others around. I tried to stand up to him and that . . . well, let's just say it didn't work. After he left again, I kept dreaming he was still there. I could hear him yelling."

He broke off talking, and we just ran for a while.

Then suddenly he said, "More than anything else, I'm afraid of ending up like him. I've got his genes."

"You're nothing like him, Tony. You must have your mom's genes."

He brightened. "Yeah, you might be right. I don't look anything like him. He's big and I'm little. He flunked out of high school. I'm going to college. Every day I tell myself I can be different from him. I *am* different from him." But he still sounded unsure.

"Sure you are."

We picked up speed. Running past lit windows, we saw kids doing homework or watching TV, parents working around the house or reading newspapers. It was almost eight-thirty. A crescent moon was barely visible in the dark sky. A breeze rattled the tree branches over our heads, and a thrill went through me. A nip in the air and football went together.

"You think we have a chance to go to the state championship this year, Tony?"

"I think so, Joey. I really do. It'll depend on our defense. Our offense is going to be outstanding."

"But Cam—"

"He's only a problem if you let him get to you."

"I keep telling myself he'll settle down. He wants to win. He won't want to hurt the team."

"He already hurts the team. In many ways." Tony clenched his jaw.

"How?"

He shook his head. "Never mind. You'll find out soon enough. It's better that you don't hate him. Yet."

"I don't really like him. How can he and I be a good team if he doesn't even talk to me?"

"Just play like a machine's throwing to you. You're better off without his friendship."

Tony probably would have laughed if he'd known I was fooling around with my hair in front of the mirror, wondering if I might look better with a Cam haircut. Maybe he'd like me better if I looked sharper. Mom had been cutting our hair since we were babies. Most of the time Logan's and my spikes looked more like tacks.

My fifteenth birthday was coming up next week. I could ask Grandpa Bobby and Grandma Heidi for a haircut if they hadn't already bought my present. If it was a choice between a new video game and having hair like a rat, I could do without the game. Or maybe Grandma Edith would buy me the haircut, though she always liked me to have something to unwrap.

"Let's push it," Tony said, picking up speed for the dash home. He pointed at the next corner. "That's where I turn off. Stay cool, and we'll be looking at that championship. Later!"

We ran on toward our separate homes. A championship! My spine tingled. And Friday I'd be playing my first game.

18

"No pressure," Dad said firmly before we left for the game. "Don't even think of us. We're invisible. Pretend we're not even there."

Grandpa Bobby and Grandma Heidi, in matching red sweaters, nodded vigorously, sending the tassel on Grandma's red cap flapping in her face. Grandma Edith mumbled behind her red scarf, wondering if I wouldn't be cold in my uniform.

"Nah, I'll be good. It's not even that cold. Besides, we wear our jackets when we're not on the field. And we have heaters."

I doubted I'd feel cold if it were ten below zero. My adrenaline had already kicked in and we hadn't even left for the game.

P.S. had gone gah-gah with excitement, wearing a red Bulldog shirt and pointing to Dad's matching shirt, the binoculars around every neck but his, the red tassel, the red scarf, and every red sweater. It was as if he was discovering the world one item at a time.

Only Mom refused to come, especially since it turned out that my first game would be played on Friday the thirteenth. "As if things weren't bad enough," she muttered. "What could they be thinking to—?" She caught Dad's eye and folded her lips. After that she served dinner silently, making no comment when I hardly ate a bite. She insisted on doing the dishes alone, and came out only once—when I was leaving.

"Try not to get too . . ." Her voice trembled and she stopped talking, leaving me to puzzle over what I wasn't to get "too." Too cold? Mangled? Mixed-up? Embarrassing?

Whatever it was, I hugged her and promised I wouldn't get that.

"Don't worry, Mom. I'll be okay."

She didn't speak to Dad, who was standing beside me. He held P.S. in one arm and Max's leash with his free hand. At the end of the leash, Max pranced around in his Bulldog outfit. Mary Pat had already picked up Logan, and through the open garage door, I saw our grandparents piling into Grandpa's car.

I was wearing my new jersey; the crew had given it to me yesterday. After the game tonight, we would turn the jerseys in and be given fresh replacements before the next game. We wore our red home jerseys tonight; the color of our visiting jerseys would vary, depending on the home team's colors. I was number 80, Jerry Rice's number. It gave me chills knowing it had belonged to one of the greatest pro wide receivers.

Mom and Dad stood in leaden silence, not quite looking at each other. We got in the car, Dad started the ignition, and we backed out, following Grandpa out the driveway. As the garage door started to lower, we saw Mom standing there alone, watching us go.

Crunch time. Hands together. "BULLDOGS!"

"Try not to tremble too much out there," Cam said in my direction. "And if you miss my passes, at least try to bat the ball to the ground before the other team can intercept."

"Cram it, Cam!" Tony snapped, lined up behind me for our charge from the locker room.

"Threatening me, half-pint?"

"It's okay, Tony," I muttered. "Forget it."

I ran from the locker room with the rest of the team. Helmets on, we rushed behind bareheaded Cam through the cheerleaders' tunnel and what seemed to be dozens of pompoms. Charging like a rampaging bull, I never lifted my head, but I knew Ashley was in the pack, her voice blending into the shrill yells from the other cheerleaders and the packed stands.

I caught a glimpse of Max frolicking toward the sidelines beside Nancy as the cheerleaders ran to face the roaring crowd. As the two male cheerleaders began their acrobatics, I looked up, searching for my family. All of them, including P.S., were waving pompoms and "Bull" dogs on sticks.

Butterflies floated in my stomach as I went through warm-up exercises and drills. I tried not to think about Dad up in the stands watching my every move with binoculars. I hadn't told him that I was most likely starting receiver. Maybe I wouldn't be, I thought almost hopefully after I missed the third practice pass. Coach might decide to start Tommy after all.

Nobody in my family expected me to play. Dad had told me not to let sitting on the bench bother me; I was new to the team. Some game soon the coach would let me in for a few plays. My grandparents had been quick to agree, probably because they remembered my years on the Little League bench.

When they saw the size and muscles of the Countryside Wildcats, they probably hoped I wouldn't play. The Wildcats came from a rural area and could lift us up and slam us down without any more trouble than throwing around bales of hay.

"Concentrate, Eastland," Coach Miller said. "If you're thinking about the mechanics of catching a ball, you won't be able to think about being nervous."

"Right. Thanks, Coach." The advice helped. By the time we finished the basic drills, I was catching Cam's routine passes.

Before I knew it Cam and Brady were walking onto the field for the coin toss. The referee flipped the coin, and Cam leaned over to look, turned, and gave us a thumb's up. His supernatural powers had worked again. We'd be receiving.

Tony caught the kickoff return and ran back fifteen yards before some gorilla tackled him on the thirty-yard line.

"Eastland!" Coach called as the offense started onto the field. "Over here!" He clapped a hand to my shoulder and leaned toward me. Out here, he didn't look anything like a middle-aged Spanish teacher. He looked like he could crack heads.

"Yeah, Coach?"

Cam ran past us onto the field, glaring at me over his shoulder.

"On running plays, you're going to have to be very aggressive in your blocking. We haven't had a chance to work on that much, but the Cats have a couple of big tough corners out there, and we need you to lay some good licks on them. If we can't find Tony some running space, he'll be dead in the water."

He pointed toward Attila the Hun, Wildcat number 17. Attila's real name was Wade Malone. I'd read about him in the local paper's high school sports columns. He was a wicked cornerback, and I might have to help hold him back if Tony was to make any yardage.

"I'll do my best," I said, trying to sound confident.

"Watch him," Coach said. "And good luck out there."

As soon as Coach released me, Tony dragged me onto the field. "What did he say?"

"Last minute instructions for the greenhorn," I said, running toward the team huddle. "He thinks I'm soft and probably a little stupid."

"He knows you're not stupid," Tony grinned. "But soft? Maybe."

"You want your head cracked?"

Tony looked over at Attila. "That big sucker looks ready to do the job."

"They all look like giants," I said. "Listen, Tony, if you can't run around them, try ducking under their legs."

He glanced toward the ambulance. "I hope they keep that thing turned on and ready to roll."

Being in the middle of the field was like being sealed in

the middle of a pounding drum. Roars came at me from both sides as the band joined with the cheerleaders in a loud cheer, the crowd adding to the discordant blare. Max pranced around with the cheerleaders, dressed in his red T-shirt, red anklets, and ribbons. Ashley was being flipped in the air by the guy cheerleaders. I still couldn't believe that such a beautiful girl had been flirting with me a little.

I tried to find Sam on the bleachers. She'd promised to watch tonight's game, too. There weren't any animals with her tonight. She said she was too nervous to fool with them. But I couldn't find her in that mass of fans.

"Okay!" Cam said in the huddle. "Spread left, dog Z motion out on three. If you can't catch it, Eastland, nobody does, got it?"

All this meant a play-action pass to me in the flat, meaning a fake handoff followed by a short pass toward the sidelines. I either had to catch it or knock it down or out of bounds so nobody else could grab it.

I shot one last look at the stands and saw P.S. standing on his seat cheering, with his little arms straight up in the air. Dad had his binoculars trained right on me. The grand-parents were all beating their hands together. All of a sudden I spotted Sam and her mom. They were sitting in front of my family, huddled together and looking spooked. Sam's fingers were in her mouth. My stomach flew into my throat. *Don't make such a big deal out of it,* I told myself.

We lined up and George White got ready for the snap. The whistle sounded. As in a dream, I heard Cam's shrill shout: *Hut! Hut! Hut!!!*

This was it. My first play in my first game.

* * *

The snap was clean and I went into motion, running my out pattern. With two different crowds yelling from both sides of the stadium, I looked over my shoulder and saw giant arms in the air between the ball and me. I yelled and jumped forward, swatting the ball away. Instead of an interception, the ball ended up on the ground. Incomplete.

Cam was glaring at me when we got back in the huddle. "That was supposed to be a five-yard out!" he snapped.

"Joey did a good job breaking it up!" Tony shot back at him. "Or you'd have had an interception."

"Who's quarterbacking this team?" Cam asked.

"You are, Cam," Melvin Barr said, surprisingly curt. "But cut him some slack. This is a good 'D' we're playing against."

I could hardly believe my ears. Brian had encouraged me during practice. Now Melvin was sticking up for me. Even tackle Jackson Allen was nodding.

Cam glared furiously around the huddle, but time was running out.

"Tight right, Z-3, stretch on two," he muttered, giving a quick, hard-nosed glance toward the packed bleachers.

Matt must be up there someplace, watching the game and wanting me to fail. He must have loved that last play. I could almost feel him smirking.

Forcing Matt from my mind, I lined up in the slot. This play was a quick pass to me over the middle. I'd already run the play against our own defense enough to know I could take a hard hit. I had a black and blue hip to remind me. *It's over the middle,* the coach had told me, *that a receiver finds out what he's made of.*

George White took the ball and got ready for the play action on two.

"*Hut! Hut!*" Cam yelled.

I was off and running. Every Wildcat thug had one agenda: to cream me.

The linebackers were the tallest and meanest of the lot and I was in their territory. If they'd had crowbars, they probably wouldn't have thought twice before using them.

I broke hard over the middle into an open seam behind the backers. A second later the ball ripped toward me. The play called for a crisp pass, but this one looked like it could burn the gloves off my fingers.

The ball slammed into my hands. I gritted my teeth and hung onto it as bodies crushed me from all sides. It was the roar from the crowds that told me I had actually held on to the football. It was only a six-yard play, but what a tough six yards.

Number 28 rolled off me and heaved himself to his feet. He leaned down and offered me a hand the size of a chuck roast. "Save yourself and stay outta my real estate next time, 80," he said, dragging me up and taking a look at my number.

The crowd kept screaming, cheering for the Bulldogs. For the first time in my life, I felt *connected*. It felt better than I'd ever dreamed it could. The next play ended my euphoria. I ran a bad pattern, and the ball was intercepted.

The Bulldogs' fans groaned while the other side went wild. Heaving myself onto the bench, I avoided all eyes and thought I'd be hearing those Wildcat cheers in my dreams later that night.

Tony sat down beside me and slapped me lightly with his towel. "You got that over with. Now it's done. Think tough."

Looking farther down on the bench, I saw Cam's mixed expression. He hated the turnover. It was bad for his stats and bad for the team. But there was also a look of grim satisfaction on his face as he nodded defiantly at someone in the bleachers.

Neither Coach Miller nor Coach Stanley came up to me. Not a single player other than Tony said a thing, though a few dark stares were aimed my way.

But I looked up to see Dave Louden standing in front of me with a water bottle. I managed a smile, remembering my own days of handing water to a dispirited player, and took the bottle. "Thanks, Dave. I need it."

Not that I felt much better. I hoped Tony was right that I had it out of my system. Fiercely, I vowed to catch anything in my range. Or if I couldn't reach it, I had to break up the play. Be a linebacker, bat at the ball, do something, anything, to keep possession.

Fortunately our defense held tough and all they got out of it was a field goal. On the kickoff we returned the ball to the thirty-five yard line and our offense took the field.

The coach called a pass for our first play. I knew he wanted to get the jitters out of me fast.

Cam threw. The ball was dead-on straight at me.

I caught it and ran and heard the cheers of the crowd over the *umphs* as bodies collided and a linebacker hurdled at me, grabbing my legs. Feeling myself fall, I threw myself forward, inched the ball out, and hit the ground. Out of breath, still holding the ball, I waited for the linebacker to get off me, then hauled myself up. The referees ran in with the chains. First down! Somehow I had inched the ball forward just far enough.

Brian Freeman dashed by on his way to the huddle. "Way to go!"

Ignoring the pain in my bruised hip, I followed him on a tear.

We were revved up now. Tony's thirty-yard burst for a TD put us up 13-10 by halftime, I had made some tough catches for good yardage, but also dropped a couple of passes. Luckily Brady was perfect with an extra point and two field goals, and our defense had two turnovers. I threw several awkward blocks, a couple of which actually worked, freeing Melvin Barr for two key runs. We weren't exactly torching them on offense, but at least we had no more turnovers.

And nobody had used the ambulance yet.

In the locker room I got my share of hand slapping as the players celebrated the first half. Until Coach Miller showed up with an attitude and blew his whistle for quiet.

"We haven't won *anything* yet," he said. "We're one score up. That can be gone in one runback. Every man is to keep his attention on business. The time for celebrating is after we get the job done."

Coach Stanley gathered our offense and started reading notes off a clipboard, lecturing us about execution and aggression and making sure we understood who was to handle which defensive Wildcat under what set of circumstances.

Coach Miller met with the defense. Later he came over to my locker and put one foot on the bench.

I looked at him, waiting to be creamed for causing the interception that had cost us three points, for running two horrible patterns and several marginal ones, and for missing at least three passes that I should have caught.

Instead he simply said, "Nice blocking out there."

I did a double take. "*Blocking*? Me, Coach? I probably looked nuts out there. I haven't really had time to practice it."

"You didn't know what you were doing, but you had guts to spare. I knew you could catch and run. I didn't know how you'd be in crunch time on the grid. A good block can win a football game."

I gulped. "Thanks."

He drank some coffee out of his thermos and started to go. Then he turned back. "Don't let up. This next half could get ugly."

Practically from the first minute of the second half, I saw what he meant. The Wildcats came out pumped. They weren't about to give up any easy points in the second half.

Their only problem was that the Bulldogs were on a major rush. Somehow, through the kind of magic that can only happen on the field, we had become believers. We knew we could pull off a major upset. And the Wildcats were beginning to believe it, too.

Stop dreaming and pay attention! So ordered the GR.

Pretty soon Cam was threading the needle to any

location on the field. His spirals were tight, timed to my run. Tony looked to be outracing jet planes. Melvin muscled a ball into the end zone, dragging a linebacker behind him. Brady was kicking for the moon.

And I started to believe I could catch greased lightning bolts.

Excitement heated the crowd into a frenzy.

Every time I looked into the stands, Dad and my grandparents were celebrating. Logan waved his shaker from the band section. Samantha and her mom hugged each other and cheered, waving pompoms. And P.S., who couldn't get his jaw to close, sat on Dad's lap with an open-mouthed smile from Lakewood to Cincinnati.

In an offensive shootout, the Wildcats roared back in the third quarter to take the lead, and we hit back just as fast. Ahead by two, we held our focus. Cam read my patterns perfectly and hit me in stride every time.

The crowd was so fired up that when a holding call took a TD from Cam and me, some guy ran onto the field screaming and had to be dragged off by security. He'd had more than a few drinks, anyone could tell. I was ashamed to see that he was wearing a Bulldog's sweatshirt.

"Forget that jerk," Cam said coldly when he saw me looking. "We've got the lead. Now let's put this game away."

It happened on the next play, with three minutes left on the clock. With Cam scrambling and our guys blocking, I ran a deep sideline pattern and beat the corner bad. But the ball was underthrown and I had to compete with the Cats' streaking safety. We both went up for it, but I outjumped him, snatched the ball inches from his fingertips, and then wheeled and ran for the goal line.

The second I crossed into the end zone, the stands exploded. Band instruments blared. I had just scored my first touchdown.

Less than three minutes later, we had the victory. Friday the thirteenth had turned out lucky for me after all. While the team celebrated on the field, I had to run for the locker room. Not that I wasn't happy and in the celebrating mood.

It was just that I was sick to my stomach.

19

I walked into the Chocolate Shoppe of Horrors with Tony, defensive lineman Diego Silva, safety Ed Bent, cornerback Brandon Hayes, and Melvin Barr, who had given us all a ride in his minivan. Cam, Matt, and the Doogan brothers had walked in just ahead of us. Several booths were already filled with players and cheerleaders. Coats and jackets were laid across two tables and another booth, reserving them for the team.

A sea of faces looked at us and cheered.

Seeing the team mainly settling at the reserved tables, I had no idea where to sit. It sure couldn't be with Cam and Matt, who were at the largest table beside Nancy and Ashley. With Matt's arm around her shoulders, Ashley caught my eye and smiled playfully, making my stomach feel like I had just swallowed a bunch of leaping frogs.

Logan jumped up from a table of band members, including Perry Toomey who frowned at me.

"Well done!" Logan said with a wide smile, clapping me on the shoulder. Mary Pat threw her arms around me, making sure everyone recognized she was in our inner circle before the two of them went back to their table.

144

I hovered awkwardly in the center of the room. Tony, more used to fame, nudged me with his elbow and pointed. Sam was waving at us from a booth in the back, her jacket spread over the seats to save them.

Just then I saw Brian Freeman start toward Cam's table. He caught my eye, jerking his chin at an empty chair, but a quick glance at Cam and Matt's scowling faces would have made up my mind even if I wasn't already headed toward Sam.

"Come on," I muttered to Tony.

"Right behind you." He grinned, and I noticed that somehow he had acquired a girlfriend in the three seconds I hadn't been watching. Alice Boone, who topped out at five feet, was now holding his hand. We all slid into Sam's booth, and the way Tony and Alice snuggled together and grinned at each other behind their menus told me this was not a first date.

Alice smiled across at me. "You guys were great tonight."

"And in tomorrow's sports column you'll read about the Bulldogs' new wide receiver—and their half-pint halfback," Tony said. "Some nickname, huh? But it doesn't bother me. I'll keep my scrapbook the rest of my life. You oughta start keeping one, too, Joey. You're gonna be mentioned a lot!"

Suddenly I felt ravenously hungry. I picked up the menu.

"Tonight's a special night," Sam said. "I guess you could have, say, twenty fries. Maybe both buns. But you can forget that hot fudge sundae."

I bopped her with the menu.

Across the Shoppe, Cam and Matt were leaning back in their chairs and howling. I wondered what the joke was. But when I glanced over, my gaze froze on Ashley. She smiled and gave me a small secretive wave.

Sam yanked on my shirt. I turned back around to find myself staring right into her eyes.

"Don't let her make an idiot of you," she said. "Especially not tonight."

"Why tonight in particular?"

"Because," she said in her serious way, "you were terrific tonight. Doing what you did wasn't easy with everyone staring at you and wondering if you were going to lose it. I was . . ." She hesitated, and her cheeks got red. "I was proud of you, Joey. You came through."

Alice slid her napkin and a pen across the table.

"What's this for?" I asked blankly.

"Sign it. Who knows?" She grinned, tongue in her cheek. "It could be worth something in about—"

"Forty years," Sam finished dryly. "No more compliments. He's had so much praise his head won't fit into his helmet."

I was trying not to look at Ashley, trying not to imagine myself being written up in the paper. It took a minute to realize that Tony was talking to me.

"I thought I'd get my dog at the Humane Society tomorrow. You up to going with me?"

"Sure. Let's try to find a dog that looks like you. How about a dachshund? Short legs, big ears, close to the ground."

"Good idea," Tony said good-humoredly. "Max looks something like you. Wrinkled pushed-in face, freckles, wags his tail when he runs . . ."

I laughed with the others and wished Max was in the car right now, waiting for a burger. But Dad had taken him home.

"We'll go tomorrow for sure," I agreed, wondering when I was ever going to get any homework done.

20

No matter how many times I went to the Humane Society, the same feeling always struck me. Seeing hundreds and hundreds of animals, all needing homes, just flattened me. I could see it knocked the breath out of Tony, too.

"How do you choose who gets to live and who has to die?" he muttered as he walked from cage to cage.

So far he had loved a spaniel mix puppy, a purebred greyhound, a collie mix, a sheltie with half a tail, a Spitz mixed with something Mom thought might be poodle, and a bunch of dogs of every description, all terrific.

Still, something made him keep going back to one little white terrier mix with black spots and a black circle around his right eye. We had Mom take him into the visiting room.

"Look how he never takes his eyes off me," Tony said as Mom set the dog down.

The terrier inched closer to Tony and dropped his head on his shoe. I knew all the signs. Tony had that sappy expression on his face that Mom called the "found-my-dog" look. "I love the mask around his eyes," he said. "And his black feet. And the way his tail wags when I pick him up. This dog is crazy about me. I can feel it."

"Great dog," Mom said. She had come in on her day off to help Tony and me. We'd been at it for over an hour, with her pointing out likely candidates as we went through every cage, looking for The Dog. Her awkwardness toward me had totally disappeared here at the shelter.

"So are you naming him LT?" I asked. The terrier was lying on the floor with his chin still on Tony's sneaker. It seemed to me that Society pets loved their humans more than any other animals did. It was as if they knew they had been saved from the executioner.

When I leaned down and picked him up, his head whipped around looking for Tony.

Tony laughed. "Nope. His name's Bandit, and he knows he's mine." He lifted him out of my arms. Bandit immediately snuggled his head into Tony's neck.

"He'd already been neutered when he came to us," Mom said, "but there's a ten dollar and fifty cent license fee and a sixty-five dollar adoption fee that includes deworming and shots. And you'll need a collar and leash, toys, and food and water bowls."

Tony waved his wallet. "I've been saving money from my paper route for six months. I have a collar and leash with me, and plenty of toys and bowls at home. Mom said it would be okay."

"Do you have her written permission?" Mom asked, all business.

"Yes ma'am. Joey said I'd need it." He fished in his pocket for the sheet of paper. Then he had to fill out a form, answering questions about how the dog would be cared for. Bandit never left his lap the whole time.

"May I call your mom to verify?"

Tony gave her the number. Mom called and talked to Mrs. Gilmore, looked the form over, and took Tony's payment. Then she lifted a nervous and whimpering Bandit from Tony's arms and carried him to the vet for his tags and a final checkup, the dog looking dejectedly over her shoulder as they left the room.

"Only problem is," Tony said while we waited, "I couldn't take them all. I hate leaving them here. Any of them."

"Since we have eight animals, plus Max, I guess we feel the same."

Mom came back out with Bandit, who immediately began struggling to get to Tony. She scratched the back of his head and handed him over, along with his vaccination papers, adoption packet, and license tag. "He was on the termination list. You saved a life today. Good job."

Tony's arms tightened around Bandit as Mom disappeared into the back. "Let's go introduce Bandit to Max."

I squirmed a little self-consciously. "Not right now."

"Why not?"

"I have to go someplace first."

"Can I go with you?"

"I'm not sure they let dogs in hair salons," I told him.

As it turned out, they were crazy about dogs in Visible Changes. They loved Bandit's black-and-white spotted hair. A lot more than they loved mine.

Ethan, the stylist, was obviously not impressed with Mom's talent with scissors. "The good part is," he said, "there's plenty of hair to work with. I think I can save you."

"What's wrong with his hair?" Tony asked, taking a better look at his own.

Ethan shuddered. "What's right with it?"

He wanted to put in blond streaks, but my birthday gift from Grandma Edith barely covered the cut and a tip, seeing as how she'd insisted on buying me a scrapbook for my football clippings as well as the haircut. When he finished cutting, I looked pretty sharp. I also had less hair on my head than I'd had since I was born.

"You realize *I* could have shaved your head if I'd known that was the look you were after," Tony said as we left the salon.

But Ethan had delivered. The proof was two girls who smiled at me just on the short walk to our bikes.

"Yeah, you're a male model all right," Tony said disgustedly as he caught me checking myself out in a window. "You have to be an idiot to pay somebody fifty bucks to cut your hair. That's crazy."

"I thought you liked it."

"I'm just wondering about something, that's all."

"What?"

"Well . . ." His face was serious; his eyes watched me closely. "Are you gonna screw on a new head if Cam says you need one?"

"Get stuffed," I said. "Cam didn't tell me I needed a haircut."

"I heard he told you it looked like a dead rat was lying on your head."

"That was Perry Toomey. Anyhow I like this haircut." I caught his quizzical look. "What? What are you thinking?"

"I'm just glad you have to wear a helmet when you play. Otherwise the hair could be a major problem. You might get it messed up on a play and start to cry out there."

"Stop it, Tony. I mean, get off it *now*!"

But he stepped closer to me, getting in my face. "Just remember this, Joey. There isn't anything on Earth that Cam would like better than changing you. He's already made you get a fifty-dollar haircut without your even knowing he did it. And he can change you in other ways. Ways you can't even imagine."

"Like how?" I asked a little uncertainly.

"You'll see, soon enough. Since he couldn't get you thrown off the team, he'll do the next best thing. He'll put his mark on you. He hasn't even begun yet."

When we walked in my house, Logan was sitting at the dining table, hunched over a newspaper. He looked up and exclaimed, "Wow!"

"Wow what?" I said blankly.

Logan pointed down to the newspaper, and he, Tony, and I crowded around it. It was open to the sports section. As I read, my heart suddenly started racing.

LAKEWOOD – The Bulldogs have got themselves a new wide receiver. Not a substitute player or a tight-end lining up in receiver position. They've got a real wide receiver.

His name is Joseph Eastland, a sophomore at Lakewood High who didn't make the team when he tried out this year. By the way, he didn't make it last year either. That would appear to be an impossibility, given that Eastland looks like he was born to catch and run. His body is built for the position, over six-one, I understand, and still growing. But it is a fact. Granted, Eastland made mistakes during the game. Granted, his blocking was weak. But he's going to get better.

"He's going to be dynamite," Coach Miller said when I caught up to him after Lakewood's 40-31 upset over the Countryside Wildcats. "He's a scrapper and he's not afraid to put himself on the line. Two years from now, it will be interesting to see how far he's come."

It'll be interesting, all right. I might sound as naïve as a rookie reporter, but I'm no rookie. I've been here fourteen years, and I've never seen a player who interested me more than this kid.

Put Eastland together with Lakewood's quality quarterback, Cameron McKey, their terrific little half-pint halfback, Tony Gilmore, and last season's all-star fullback, Melvin Barr, and you have a lot to talk about. And I didn't even mention Ambrose Morse, their impressive tackle, Brian Freeman, better known as Mr. Freeze for his cool head at tight end, and a very good defense led by dominant linebacker Ricardo Gonzalez. We also didn't mention Ed Bent, one of the tallest and best safeties I've seen at the high school level. Add to that their kicker, Brady Hanson, who must be exciting the college scouts with his whopping 92 percent field goal kicking from thirty yards or less, and Lakewood starts looking like a real contender.

After more than ten years without a single appearance in the Division Two championship playoffs, the Lakewood Bulldogs might just be more than a contender this season. They may be the team to beat.

"We have a very good team," Coach Miller said. "And Eastland may be our last missing link."

I'll second that.

BY BRAD HOLTZMAN
LAKEWOOD GAZETTE STAFF

I looked up with blurred eyes and felt the words garble in my throat as I mumbled, "I can't believe it."

Logan looked like he could hardly believe it either.

But Tony grinned. "Hate to say I told ya so!" he said.

Over the next couple of hours the phone kept ringing. Every time I grabbed the receiver, I hoped it was somebody from the loop. But it was either Sam or Dad or my grandparents. Even Ted Wyatt from the project called, offering congratulations in his usual shy voice that gave no hint of his own local celebrity.

Ricardo Gonzalez and Melvin Barr called from the team, but there was no word from Cam or any of his group.

I looked in the mirror and was glad I had my new haircut. Maybe the article, plus the haircut, plus spending more time with the team and playing more games would do the trick.

"Just can't keep your eyes off yourself, can you?" Tony

grinned. "Personally, I liked you better with all that fuzz on your head. It covered the point."

Everybody but Tony thought my new haircut was terrific. Later that night Mary Pat came over to coach Logan for his SATs. After congratulating me enthusiastically on my write-up, she said that if Logan were thinner, she'd love for him to get his hair cut like mine. "But on a chubby person, it just wouldn't work," she said. "See what I mean?"

Tony and I glanced up from the floor where we were bouncing balls for our dogs. Bandit had grabbed the first forty or so, but who was counting? He had also run circles around Max in the backyard and learned how to retrieve, as well as do Max's begging trick. But Max didn't seem to mind. He was content just to sink his head onto my leg as I looked at Mary Pat's drawing.

She had sketched a small head with something resembling my haircut on it. It was set on such a huge, flabby body that it looked like a pinhead.

"It's all a matter of balance," she said with a sigh. She passed the sketch to my brother, and he studied it with a red face.

"My body looks like a blimp on a string?" he asked her. "My head's a peanut?"

"Honey, we can disguise it. All we have to do is dress you in loose clothes so nobody suspects what's inside them, until you lose enough weight."

"Great," he said. "Just terrific. Should I maybe wear a paper bag over my head, too? We don't want anyone to see it's two inches in diameter."

Mary Pat pinched his cheeks. "But I just love your cute little head. Now forget it and let's get down to business."

"Listen, Mary Pat . . ." Logan's voice rose thickly. Tony and I froze in midbounce as Bandit grabbed another ball. I hoped that my brother was finally going to stand up for himself.

"What is it, honey bear?" Mary Pat said as if he was a child of two.

My brother glared at her.

"This might be it," I whispered to Tony. "He may finally be ready to let her have it."

"Go get 'er, Logan," Tony whispered hopefully. Bandit shoved the ball at him, wanting him to throw it again. "Wait a minute, boy, we may be watching a mutiny."

But after a very long moment of silence, my brother dropped his eyes and picked up his pencil. "Never mind," he mumbled. "Okay, show me how to do that problem again."

"Glad to, honey. You have no idea how much I love being your mentor."

Tony and I looked at each other.

"Slam-dunked again," I said.

Mom came in just as Max looked as if he was finally going to catch a ball. But it took a bad bounce and Bandit grabbed it.

"Everybody stay for dinner," she said. "We're ordering in two buckets of fried chicken." She stared at Max, who was searching everywhere, his teeth still primed for a catch. "What's he looking for?"

"The ball," I said as Max suddenly spotted it in Bandit's mouth.

His mouth sagged and he collapsed back to the floor, having given his all.

"Never mind, boy," I said, reeling him in for a hug. "You don't have to catch balls when you're a famous mascot."

At the dinner table Mary Pat started lecturing about cylinders and trapezoids. My brother desperately tried to pretend he was interested.

Which suddenly reminded me of my own neglected work. "I've hardly done any homework all week," I muttered uneasily.

"I'm trying not to get behind," Tony said. "I started off slow in middle school, when things were rough at home. I have to keep improving if I'm going to get a merit scholarship."

I thought about Dad's business and knew I'd need a scholarship, too. It would be all my parents could do to pay for Logan's tuition if he didn't get any funding. But studying was the last thing I wanted to do.

"Come on," I said. "Let's take our run."

"What? It's barely past twilight. They can still see us."

"Who cares? Let's go."

"I get it. You're looking for hair admirers."

"Get stuffed."

He got Bandit's leash. "Okay, let's go. Then I have to go home and hit the books. Come on, Bandit, the Missing Link here says it's time to run."

Max strolled uninterestedly to the door with us, but made no effort to follow. Knowing him, he would exercise by going into the kitchen after we left, hoping for another handout.

Side by side, with Bandit at Tony's heels, we ran. I promised myself that after we got back, I'd study, too. But when Tony had gone home and the last of the light had long faded from the sky, all I felt like doing was lying on the couch, staring at the ceiling and thinking about running into the end zone with a football tucked under my arm.

21

"In many Asian cultures," Sam said, "it's impolite to say no to an invitation, even if you have no intention of attending the function."

I looked up. "Really?"

"Congratulations, Samantha Burton. You have engaged Mr. Eastland's interest." Mrs. C. was her usual self—put together, sharp, and ready to point fingers and take names. She was dressed in flaming red with gold hoops in her ears. As usual she was all business. "What snagged you, Eastland?"

I'd actually been trying to decide how humiliated I'd feel if I asked Ashley for a date and she turned me down. I blushed. "Um . . . I was thinking that it must be hard to, uh, figure out if a person really wants to go wherever you're asking them to go."

"They understand, but we wouldn't," Sam explained, not realizing that "a person" was Ashley. "Because we don't know their customs. It's also polite in some cultures to say 'no' several times when you're offered food, before eventually saying 'yes'. If you weren't familiar with their etiquette, you might not keep asking, and your guests would all leave hungry, thinking how rude you had been."

Sam had a glossary of gestures, including the Texas Longhorn sign, made by holding up your fist while leaving your index finger and pinkie sticking up. But in some parts of Africa you were cursing somebody if you used this signal; in Brazil it meant good luck; and in Italy, it signified infidelity. Even in America, it had different meanings, such as "the evil eye" or a gangland sign that signified "horns of the devil."

"All of this goes to show how misunderstandings spring up across the globe," Sam concluded. "Even our body language can be misread."

Perry got up with what looked to be a thousand pictures of artifacts. I leaned my head on my hand and tried to keep my eyes open by reciting the playbook to myself. I caught a word here and there, all delivered in hypnotically boring tones:

". . . the importing of wine in a country that had never fermented fruit . . . the translucency of wine glasses showing the wine's color . . . square-sided glass bottles of half to one-liter capacity for olive oil from the Mediterranean region . . ."

Wake up, I warned myself, feeling that Perry could get a job in a sleep clinic, lulling chronic insomniacs into REM and holding them there until they went comatose.

"Very nice, Mr. Toomey. That leaves us with Mr. Eastland, who will help us to better understand how sports have both united the world and split us apart."

Half out of my seat, I sat down again, not having exactly considered my presentation in such terms. I had planned to bombard Mrs. C. with *facts,* like descriptions of the first sports played at the Olympics, and how the early games had begun with a truce between those gathered to watch the contests.

"You are ready, I presume, Eastland?"

"Yes ma'am," I lied.

"Please proceed."

I glanced down uneasily at the sheaf of papers in my hand.

"Mr. Eastland?"

I took a deep breath and put myself into my most dynamic mode. Obviously last week I had failed to make it clear how very dramatic and terrifying chariot races and racing on unsaddled horses could be for the *people* involved. The people were what she was interested in. I moved from equestrian events to boxing, wrestling, pankration, running, jumping, discus, and javelin.

I felt sure I brought boxing to life in all its horrors: an endless bout without rounds and essentially without rules, lasting until one opponent was either unconscious or admitted defeat. Then came wrestling, where breaking your opponent's fingers was legal. Pankration was a ruthless combination of wrestling and boxing, with only biting and gouging out your opponent's eyes forbidden.

"Kicking your opponent in the belly was perfectly legal," I said, hoping to hear shocked gasps.

Instead I was annoyed to see Perry stifling a yawn and

161

the two artists doodling idly. Sam, who had taken notes through Perry's entire boring presentation, was leaning back in her seat without even a pen in her hand.

Mrs. C. sat at her desk, staring at me expressionlessly as I began a lengthy discussion of the various Olympian races. At least both artists glanced up when I mentioned the two to four stade races run by athletes in full armor—a stade being the distance across the stadium. Yet when I finished, the only sound was the faint scratch of drawing pencils sketching on paper.

"How did they enforce fair play in these contests?" Mrs. C. asked after pursing her lips in thought for a moment.

"Well, they . . . they . . ." I swallowed and ran my finger down the page. Not finding the exact answer, I did the best I could. "There were no weight divisions. Opponents were chosen randomly. A man weighing a hundred and fifty pounds could end up fighting a man over two hundred. Their heads got so beaten up that Plato called boxers 'the folk with the battered ears.'"

"Was the crowd empathetic to the terrible injuries?" Mrs. C. asked.

I knew she had begun to guide me like I was a helpless child, but there was no option but to continue. "Actually, the more brutal the better. The crowds loved the violence."

"Perhaps this love of violence led to rougher games and eventually maybe even the gladiatorial games?"

"It could be." I shuffled through my papers. "Ah . . . wait, gladiators . . ."

"Excellent, I see you are prepared to speak of them. Please proceed."

I was reluctant to burn next session's planned gladiatorial presentation by tacking it onto today's work, but nevertheless I began to read rapidly: "About 264 BCE, the first gladiator games started with three pairs of slaves selected from twenty-two prisoners of—"

"Put your notes aside, please, Mr. Eastland. We were speaking of how the Olympian crowds enjoyed violence. Was this also true of those watching gladiator contests? And did the crowd have favorites and like one gladiator while perhaps disliking his opponent?"

"Yes ma'am."

"Did the gladiators hate and wish to kill each other?"

Relieved that I actually had an interesting answer, I explained that they didn't. "Though gladiators occasionally killed each other in the ring, new research shows that they fought like gentlemen. It seems that while the crowd might scream for blood, the gladiators had codes of ethics among themselves. Examination of gladiators' remains shows they didn't use sneak attacks or try to inflict mortal wounds. About 90 percent of the time, both gladiators lived through a match. And if a gladiator was dying, he was taken backstage and killed with one quick hammer blow to the side of his head."

Finally Mrs. C. was nodding and smiling. "Does anyone notice a parallel here to today's world?" she asked.

Sam raised her hand hesitantly. "Well, we do separate ourselves into groups, don't we, like the gladiators versus the crowd? Street gangs against other gangs. Countries against other countries. So often when we unite, we divide ourselves from others. It's a paradox."

"Exactly. Sports are a good example of this. Being part of a team unites. But in playing games, the opposing team turns into an enemy, at least temporarily. Opposite sides sometimes hate each other."

"But we don't hope to see people on the other team get killed or knocked out," I protested.

Perry Toomey raised his hand.

"Yes, Perry?" Mrs. C. said pleasantly.

"If a team loses, their fans get into fights, smash windows, and even use weapons. Sometimes they even kill each other. Look at the violence after the soccer World Cup."

Ted Wyatt stirred. "Let's do a canvas on sports that shows what international sporting events are supposed to do. Bring us together, not tear us apart."

Kelsey nodded. "I like the image of men running in their armor inside a stadium. Our theme could be that though sports might look like war, they are meant to unite us. The armor could be a symbol of how hard it is to keep our perspective. We could call it The Great Paradox."

The warning bell dinged, and Mrs. C. beckoned me as the others left.

"If it gets us another painting, I'll let you off," she said quietly. "But you have a ways to go yet, both in our project and in your classwork for me. I hope you're keeping up better in your other subjects."

The look on my face must have told her all she needed to know.

"I see. Listen, Eastland, it's time to take care of business—off the field as well as on. Will you make that commitment?"

I gazed back at her uncertainly. But I nodded.

"Good." Her face relaxed and she suddenly chuckled. "By the way, I saw you play your first game. You were *bad,* baby! You had those Wildcats talking to themselves."

"I would have thought you'd hate making your opponent feel terrible," I said curiously.

"I never claimed that I wasn't human, Mr. Eastland. If we are to understand others' paradoxes, we had better admit we have them ourselves!"

When I walked out the door, she was still sitting at her desk and laughing. I could hear her out in the hallway.

Perry was waiting. He grabbed me before Sam had the chance. "We have the DNA quiz this morning," he said, looking anxious. "Are you ready for it? Have you studied your genetic terms?"

I stared at him blankly. "The quiz is this morning? Are you sure?" My stomach tightened at the look on his face. One honors class after the other loomed ahead of me like minefields, but this one was by far the worst. There could be no faking scientific terms.

"Listen, Perry—"

"I don't have time to listen." He began aiming questions at me, making me feel more seriously ill with every one: "What is a gene? An allele? What does it mean to be phenotypically dominant?"

The only one I knew was "gene."

165

"What is homozygous recessive?"

"A cow that does her own homogenization?"

"This is not funny," Perry said stiffly. His face was paler than ever, his pimples more pronounced. "If you flunk this test, it will look bad for me as well as for you."

"Why?"

"Because we're supposed to be partners. He'll assume we're working together." Perry was following some deep thread of reasoning that was reducing him to helpless panic. He hovered beside me in the hall, grilling me and scribbling lists of genetic groupings to study. Only when the warning bell sounded did he scamper toward his homeroom.

Luckily we had French class together. He sat beside me, passing me practice quizzes he had hastily composed in homeroom and handing them back corrected in broad, angry strokes.

Too soon, we were walking into biology. He was still snapping questions at me, but broke off in a squeak as Mr. Adams handed each of us a test and motioned us to our table.

Seeing that he was watching me with fear almost as terrible as my own, I tried to look confident as I skimmed a quiz paper that was chock-full of terms and genetic codes. If I hadn't already felt nervous, feeling Perry trembling beside me would have done the trick. The more he shivered, the shakier I got.

Finishing just at the bell, I laid my paper on the top of the stack and hoped that I had somehow, with Perry's help, managed to do just enough cramming to pass.

He dogged my heels in the line heading for the door. "Well?"

I shrugged. "I think about a C. At least I hope so."

"You *hope* you got a C?" His face looked awful. He turned away abruptly, having caught sight of Mr. Adams coming back into the room.

"Could I have a word with you, sir?"

"Of course," our teacher said courteously. "What can I do for you, Perry?"

He slunk into the room, hovering over Mr. Adams's desk and refusing to look at me. He was talking very fast, his face pleading, and I realized what he was up to. The incredible fink was asking to change lab partners.

22

"That haircut makes even a face like yours passable," Cam told me the next morning before school. "Now if you only had better sneakers and some name-brand clothes."

Matt was off suspension now and back in Cam's group, leaning against the wall.

"You talk to the coach?" Roddy Doogan was asking Matt as I passed them.

Curious, I hovered at the outskirts of the group, glancing sideways at Matt's furious face while thumbing through my history book.

"He says there's nothing he can do," Matt complained. "It's over his head. Such bull. All this, thanks to that little twerp." He glowered, and gestured over at Perry, who was just walking in the front door with a rolled-up poster under one arm and two bulging backpacks, one slung over each shoulder.

"We could plant an answer sheet on him and turn *him* in for cheating," Cam suggested.

"We couldn't even *write* a good enough cheat sheet to plant on him," Matt said gloomily. "He'd probably write his cheat sheet in Latin. Besides, who'd believe he needs one?"

"Whatever happens," Cam said, "has to be done off school grounds. Or the rest of us could get suspended."

"Thanks for the support," Matt growled.

"I'm supporting you," Cam said edgily. "But I don't want to get thrown off the team, too."

"How about if we spray painted Tombstone's house?" Roddy suggested.

"Not after that graffiti stuff we got caught doing to the gas station," his brother reminded him. "They'd call in the cops."

"How I'd like to knock that smug little nose right off his face," Cam said as Perry passed by, head raised loftily. The whole group followed him, calling out mocking insults and leaving me to stare blankly into my book.

"What's up?" Sam suddenly appeared beside me wearing a blue sweater and some new, tight jeans. Her hair was shorter and styled to curve around her chin. I noticed Brady Hanson looking at her over his shoulder as he trailed Cam's group.

"Nothing," I said, part of me wishing they would spray paint Perry from head to toe. Yet I knew I should do something. Suddenly I remembered that Brady had said nothing during that discussion. Neither had Tommy Brink or George White. Maybe it was just talk.

She smiled up at me. "You want to know what *I* was thinking?"

I blinked back at her. "What?"

She pointed to the glassed-in administration office in the lobby. There was a notice on the glass: Tickets for the Wacky Winter Dance are now on sale.

"It's not even fall," I said.

"You get the tickets cheaper if you buy early."

"I don't have a date."

She looked murderous. "What am I, a pickaxe?"

"We don't *date*, Sam. Besides, you don't want to go to the dance with me. You know I can't dance."

"Would you rather take Blondie?"

I knew the "Blondie" she meant.

"Okay, okay," I said. "I just got my allowance this morning. Those tickets will eat up every cent of it."

"I'll buy my own," she offered. "Since it was my idea."

I had to admit she was being fair. Ashley Parker would never have agreed to buy her own ticket. But why would she have to, with all the guys who would be waiting in line to ask her to the dance?

"And don't worry about the dancing," Sam added. "My folks are offering me lessons. I'll take them and teach you."

"Okay." It was a relief not to feel uncomfortable. We could learn together. That was the difference between dating and just going to a dance with a friend.

"By the way," Sam asked as we started to the office, "what happened to your birthday money? Are you wearing it on your head?"

"Well—"

"It's okay," she said quickly, looking over my new haircut and smiling. "It looks nice."

"Yours does, too."

She blushed. "I didn't think you'd noticed."

"Oh, well, yeah," I said. "Sure. I noticed."

We were the only ones in line for tickets. Mrs. Geller,

the office secretary, tore off two and handed them to us. "Have a wonderful time," she said, smiling at us. "I hope you don't mind my saying you make a wonderful couple."

"Thanks!" Sam beamed.

I suddenly remembered that Mary Pat had said we were a great couple, too. All at once, I couldn't quite look Sam in the eye. I studied my ticket instead. It was number six out of a roll big enough to serve as a bus tire.

"Good thing we got in early," I remarked. "They might have sold out."

"Better put your ticket away," she said, carefully tucking hers into her wallet. "You don't want to lose it."

I stuck my ticket into a packet of open gum; then, seeing her look at me, I pulled it out and put it into my zippered pen case.

"Well, I gotta get to homeroom," I mumbled. "I still have some homework." Why did I keep staring into Sam's eyes? And why did they look so pretty? It suddenly hit me that she wasn't wearing glasses.

"Sam, are you wearing . . . ?" I took a closer look at her eyes.

"Contacts. You like them?" She grinned.

"Not bad."

"Careful," she warned. "I can't handle too many compliments at one time."

"What—?"

"Never mind," she said nicely, noticing me looking at her jeans. "You see something else you like?"

"Uh . . ."

"Thank you very much!"

"Why are you smiling like that?"

"Like what?" she asked, giggling.

I looked at her, stunned, never having heard her make quite that sound before. A laugh, yes. A giggle, never.

What was going on?

23

"Where do I sit?" I asked Tombstone, walking into biology.

"Right here," he said gloomily, pointing at the seat beside him at our table. "We're still together. Mr. Adams wouldn't let me change, even though I told him I'd take practically anybody else."

"Nice of you."

He frowned at me. "I didn't request you because I wanted to partner a C student."

"Did anybody ever tell you that you could make a hog barf? And *nothing* makes a hog sick."

"I doubt that is a scientific fact," he scoffed.

I'd known Perry wasn't exactly my cup of tea. I just hadn't known I couldn't stand him. I told Tony so on the way home that afternoon.

"He's just a little eccentric. When you're that smart, you gotta be different from everybody else. Goes with the territory. Give him a break. What's he got to do with you?"

"He's making me crazy."

I pictured Perry's silly little face. I hated to sit beside him in biology. Hated being his partner. Even looking at him reminded me of an image I used to carry in my head. The one I used to be afraid I looked like.

That night I got out my kit and performed cheek swabs on my entire family, as well as Tony, Mary Pat, and the family next door. I also became the proud owner of more than a dozen test tubes of spit and a few more with animal slobber.

Carefully dividing my last cotton swab into particles and sealing each particle into a plastic baggy, I thought of flattening Perry's nose. In all my life, hitting somebody had never even occurred to me. What would happen if I really did fight him? What if I was to do the very thing that Cam and Matt were both dying to do but didn't dare? I stood still and considered: What if I could get Matt's revenge for him? I imagined Cam and his group and maybe even Ashley all looking at me in a new way.

I breathed in sharply, shocked at what I'd been thinking.

That night my dreams were confused, full of football and Perry Toomey, alternating with cheers and jeers.

I was getting ready to sock Perry in the jaw when I woke up to an earthquake. At least it sounded like one. It took me a minute, staring down at a shadowy figure sprawled on the floor, to realize that Logan had just fallen out of bed.

Max peered over the edge of the bed, whimpering. I lifted him and took him down the ladder with me. Logan looked to be gasping. I handed him his water bottle from the desk.

"Thanks," he panted. "What an awful dream."

"You, too? What was yours?"

He shuddered. "I was in the examination room taking my SATs. I felt pretty good. Then people started whispering and pointing. That's when I turned and saw Mary Pat's head. We were high up in a tall building and her head was sort of, sort of *floating* there at the window. And her neck . . ." His eyes glazed. "It looked as long as an anaconda, but thin as a hose. You could tell she wanted in!"

"What happened?"

"The teacher opened the window, and Mary Pat's head and neck came slithering in. She came right at me. Closer and closer until she was looking over my shoulder while I was marking my paper. And all of a sudden I couldn't remember how to do a single problem. My mind was blank."

"That's horrible."

"I started screaming, and that's when I woke up."

Max and I sat beside him on the floor. We'd been sharing a room since I was born. There were times when I'd wished I had it all to myself—and I'm sure he felt the same. But if he lived on campus next year, I'd miss him.

Neither of us said anything for a while, then Logan propped himself up on one elbow and looked at me. "Mary Pat," he said, "is very smart."

"Yeah."

"Maybe too smart for me."

"Mary Pat," I said, "may be too smart for anyone."

"Maybe." He started to get up, but his legs wobbled. I put out a hand and dragged him to his feet. He was more than four inches shorter than me, but he was still my big brother. He had always been there for me and it felt good to be there for him now.

"You'll work it out," I said. "Believe me, it'll be okay. Be glad you're dealing with this now, before you have four kids and a mortgaged house in Pittsburgh."

He grinned. "Good point. Thanks."

I waited until he crawled back into bed. Then I climbed back up to my bunk, Max under my arm. He snuggled in close beside me, yawning widely, his breath warm against my side. He was not much good at running or fetching, but he was a great sleep mate.

I finally fell asleep again and didn't dream the rest of the night. This time nobody fell out of bed.

24

For the first time I discovered what it was to attack school-work without inspiration. Robotically, I plowed through the week, trying to reclaim lost ground and saving the majority of my dreaming for the playing field. I got a nod from Mrs. C. for tracing as many sports as possible back to their roots, which seemed a waste of time since the instant I noted a sport's origination, I was sure to find a contradicting piece of information.

While the United Kingdom claimed cricket, rugby, and football, many French swore cricket belonged to them. Soccer was up for grabs. The Chinese had a version of it seven thousand years ago called Tsu Chu, where the players hit a fat stuffed leather ball into a hole. The three-thousand-year-old Japanese version was called Kemari, while the British claimed their soccer started when a Danish prince was beheaded and people started kicking his head around. It went on and on.

Baseball was almost as bad. Variations of it were played in Europe and America during the 1600s and even earlier by the Mayans.

Basketball, golf, table tennis, bowling, badminton . . . I kept at it, my list growing longer and more contradictory.

Sam had been assigned to foods and had found the same contradictions. She was amazed to find that the first pizzas could be traced to ancient Egypt, Greece, and Rome.

"They probably served it at the Olympics," Perry said sourly, and he seemed surprised when everyone laughed. He had been assigned to trace the origins of different kinds of music and prattled on about Vedic origins, including hymns in the Vedas, and music and instruments being mentioned in such ancient works as the Upanishads, Brahmanas, Puranas, and in epics like Ramayama and Mahabharata.

"You're so intelligent," Ted Wyatt told him admiringly, "that I can hardly understand a word you say."

He got a laugh, too. In fact lately there was a lot of laughter in "The Power of Understanding." Even Kelsey seemed lit up. She often participated in the talk, asking questions and sharing impromptu sketches.

"You see how connected we are in so many ways?" Mrs. C. asked.

"We really are," Kelsey said enthusiastically.

On Friday night Mom came in wearing her red jacket and grimly announced she had decided to go to our game with Northside High.

"I went crazy last week, not knowing what horrible things were happening. Better just to see them with my own eyes," she finished gloomily.

My grandparents' car pulled into our driveway,

Grandpa's windshield wipers making arcs in the misty rain. Thunder rumbled overhead as we headed toward the school. Looking through the rear window, I saw Grandpa bent over the wheel in a thick jacket and knit cap and caught a fainter glimpse of both grandmothers sitting together in the backseat.

"Won't they call the game?" Mom asked, chewing her lip nervously, obviously thinking of lightning bolts and weather-related accidents.

I saw a trace of impatience in Dad's face as he looked sideways at her. "Football's a tough game, Grace," he murmured. "They play in all sorts of weather. Rain, snow, fog, and freezing weather. I think they cancel for hail, tornadoes, hurricanes, earthquakes, and volcanoes, though."

She wrung her hands. "If there's lightning or even thundering, Joey, promise me you'll leave the field!"

Her words were met with silence. I sat in the back seat beside P.S. It was an away game and since Logan was not in the smaller pep band that accompanied the team, he had gone ahead of us with Mary Pat.

We pulled into Lakewood High's front parking lot and saw the bus, a huge, shadowy presence in the dim drizzle. Nerves set in. Could I play as well again, especially knowing Mom was out there, moaning at every play?

Tony came toward the car wrapped in a yellow raincoat, the hood pulled over his face. "Hi, everybody! Nice night for a game, huh?"

The knot in my stomach eased. Grinning, I jumped from the car and followed him to the bus. We climbed up after José Lopez and Ambrose Morse and found seats toward the back. The coaches sat up front behind the driver, conferring over their clipboards.

Looking back through the rain-fogged rear window, I could barely see Dad pulling from the parking lot, Grandpa driving close behind. The bus driver started the motor.

Coach Stanley stood up and checked names off his list. "Okay, let's do it!"

We were packed in together, all for one and one for all, shouting a fight cheer as the bus rumbled slowly toward the street.

Weather or not, Friday's game couldn't have gone any better. My blocking improved. I made catches right out of my own dreams and ran two of them into the end zone through the drizzling rain. Nothing could stop me. I was jumping the hurdles for real now.

After the game, Coach Miller stopped by my locker with the first solemn face I'd seen on him all night. He said, "You're going to have to stay mentally tough, Eastland. If you let this thing go to your head, you can blow a great window of opportunity. It's best to remember that you have a lot to learn. Don't pay too much attention to the kudos."

Easier said than done.

Leaving the locker room, I found a horde of people waiting for me, crowded around the snack bar and on the bleachers. My parents and grandparents, brothers, Sam, kids from the loop and out of it—everybody I knew rushed at me. Grandpa said he had never had such a night in his life.

"Sports are thrilling," he said, "but not all that good for the heart."

My dad walked around with a dazed smile on his lips, saying "Wow" over and over like it was the only word he knew.

Mom burst into tears and grabbed me, thrilled to find me in one piece. "You-were-wonderful-oh-I'm-so-glad-you're-all-right!" she sobbed, squeezing my arms and shoulders to assure herself I really was. Probably she had watched the game from between her fingers. The touchdowns were only vaguely important to her; the main thing was that I was okay.

Actually I did have a few aches and pains. But in the words of Joe Montana, "When you win, nothing hurts." It was almost true.

Despite the coach's advice, all of a sudden I was picturing myself as a college receiver. Or even a pro receiver. Who knew?

"You riding back on the bus?" Dad asked.

"Yeah. And then I'm going to the Chocolate Shoppe with some of the guys. I've got a ride."

"Fine. We'll take Max with us."

I looked at my dog, still in his mascot outfit and standing on a sheet of paper in front of the snack bar. He was surrounded by an admiring circle of kids. "What are they doing?"

"Getting paw prints. That's what comes from being featured in the paper as 'Lakewood High's Lucky Bulldog.'" Dad lifted him carefully off the paper, watching out for his inky feet. "Sorry, guys, even a mascot needs his down-time." He wiped Max's front paws with his handkerchief and then snapped on his leash. "Come on, star, let's get you home."

George White had offered me a ride to the Shoppe in his van along with Tommy, Wayne, and Brady. When I asked if Tony could come along, he hesitated, then shrugged.

"Sure, I guess so."

Somehow Brady ended up sitting beside me in the back. Halfway to the Shoppe, he turned to me. "I was gonna ask you. Is Sam your girl?"

"Well . . ." I started to say no, but I didn't like the look in his eyes. "I'm taking her to the dance, but we're not really . . ." Or were we? I was getting a little confused on that.

But Brady nodded. "Gotcha. So then she's available."

For some strange reason, I wanted to say no, but how could I, when I was planning to ask Ashley for a date? "I guess so," I agreed reluctantly.

"Great. Didn't want to step on your toes." He winked and elbowed my ribs.

The evening was a blur. Tony and I sat with Alice and Sam. Ashley shot daggers at Sam from across the room, making me wonder if she could possibly be competing with her for me. Brady had his eye on Sam, too, but with an altogether different look in his eyes.

"He looks like he's leaning over a lobster tank, trying to pick out his dinner," I complained squeamishly.

"Oh yeah?" Sam said with a smile.

I was surprised at how good it felt to be sitting next to her, and even more surprised to find myself holding her hand.

Cam yelled lazily from his table. "You know what, Eastland? We ought to let the college scouts know we'd like to go to the same college. Too bad I'll get there a year early. We'd make some package." Maybe he only said it because Matt wasn't there, but he'd said it!

Slouched against the back of the booth, my hand warm in Sam's, I gazed around at the crowded tables and found myself puzzled as to who exactly *did* make up the loop. I'd always thought of the loop as, basically, Cam and Matt, plus the best-looking, hippest, and most athletic guys— and, of course, Nancy, Ashley, most of the cheerleaders, and other beautiful girls. But looking around the room, I saw many "loopy" people sitting with the un-loopiest, many in couples and holding hands with unlikely dates. Was there really a loop at all?

I turned to look at Ashley and found her smiling back at me, and I knew there must be a loop, if only for girls like her. Whatever the case, I had the warm, completed feeling of finally being a part of it all.

Unfortunately Saturday was a new day, and I had to get up early. Dad had received a big shipment, and Logan and I had to stock shelves. I also had to walk the three dogs and feed them while Logan took care of the cats and the snakes.

When I came in for breakfast, Mom had the paper open to the local sports headlines. She shoved it at me, and I saw a picture of myself standing in drizzling rain, my white visitor's jersey streaked with mud. It was captioned: *Bulldogs' wide receiver, Joe Eastland, shows his talent on a muddy field.*

Max nudged my ankle. I had a piece of turkey bacon halfway to the floor when I froze. Max had to pry the bacon from my fingers.

"What's the matter?" Mom looked up from the shopping list she had just begun. Saturdays she caught up on housework, errands, and grocery shopping. She never really stopped.

I didn't answer, only stared at her with the blood draining from my head.

"*Joey!* I asked you what's wrong!"

"D-did you read what he said about the team?" It was hard to breathe.

Mom frowned. "What do you mean? The article's mostly about you, not the rest of the team. It mentioned Tony, too, what a good runner he is. And Cam."

"Yeah, Cam got a rave all right," I muttered. I read from the article:

Lakewood High School delivered a knockout surprise this season when Coach Miller brought in unknown sophomore Joe Eastland as his new wide receiver. Eastland's explosive talents are showcased by junior quarterback Cameron McKey, who has never looked so good thanks to Eastland's sticky fingers. The rest of what had looked to be a rather pedestrian team during its first two lackluster games contributed in efforts that brought their combined talent to more than the sum of its parts. My own personal favorite, half-pint running back Tony Gilmore, rose from the pack to shine yet again. This little kid is terrific. Linebackers and tacklers twice his size keep pounding his face into the dirt, and he keeps getting up and doing it all over again. This kid just will not quit running. If the rest of the team will play up to their best, Eastland and Gilmore could lead the Bulldogs on a championship run.

"Isn't that nice for Tony?" Mom smiled and added a few items to her list.

"Yeah, for Tony," I groaned, looking out the window. The sky, so bright only moments before when I'd walked the dogs, had turned to crud, suggesting more rain.

Mom looked perplexed. "What's wrong? I'd think you'd be six feet off the ground."

"It's what they said about the rest of the team. Cam . . ." Words failed me.

She took the paper and frowned down at the article. "It says right here that he's never looked so good."

"Because of my sticky fingers," I moaned. "Mom, he wants to be a pro quarterback. He's the leader of the team, not 'Eastland and Gilmore.' This article makes it look like he's there to showcase my talent!"

"Why are your fingers sticky?" she asked, helpless to understand why I should be so upset at such a wonderful review. "I didn't get that part. Don't you wash your hands before you play?"

Everything was fading away. Not only was Cam going to hate me, but so was the entire team. Stupid writer. At least last week he had mentioned some of the other good players. Then, looking at the byline, I saw the article was by another writer and realized that this column was from the *Sentinel,* the bigger paper.

"It's horrible," I mumbled. "Horrible, horrible, horrible."

My hands trembled so hard the newspaper rattled. My throat closed up. I put my hand to my head and felt the new haircut, trying to remember how I'd looked in the mirror before I went to bed last night. That kid had vanished like he'd never been there at all.

"Maybe you've got it totally wrong," Logan said, coming in from feeding the cats. "Maybe you're so important now that everyone will be licking your shoestrings."

The phone rang. It was Tony. "Oh, man," he said. "This is bad."

I groaned. "What kind of jerk writes an article like that about high school kids?"

"I don't know," he said furiously, "but it's the kind of thing that can rip our team apart. I have to take a shower; I just got home from my route. Later."

Immediately the phone rang again.

"Congratulations, Joey," Sam said very quietly.

I nodded dumbly at the phone and heard her sigh. "I knew you'd be feeling down about the way the stupid sportswriter put it. But aren't you at least thrilled about the article?"

I shuddered. "It—it was all about being on a team, Sam.

It was always about that. Not just being one player on the field. We're a team. I mean, we *were* a team."

"Oh, Joey," she whispered.

At the store that day I felt leaden, hardly able to move. Even Logan was faster than me.

"Are your feet nailed to the floor?" Dad asked as I lugged boxes from the back. "Finish that and then go get some more sleep."

"I'm okay," I said. "I couldn't sleep anyhow."

Logan didn't look much better than me. Dad bought us all subs for lunch and then sent us home, leaving me to get through the rest of Saturday as best I could, while Logan went to study at Mary Pat's. It would have helped if Tony could have come over, but he had a major paper due for English.

"Me, too," I said drearily. "Mine is on *The Heart Is a Lonely Hunter.*"

"With a title that good, you don't even need any words inside the cover."

Carson McCullers had some good words inside, but though my fingers thudded down heavily on the keys, I hardly knew what I was typing. I was as cut off and separate from my work as any of McCullers's lonely characters.

The paper was woefully short, only two double-spaced pages.

The phone rang. I jumped, but it was only Tony again. He seemed almost as down as I felt.

"Have you heard from anybody?" I asked, filled with dread.

"A few."

"Like who?"

"Not Cam, if that's who you mean. Melvin, José, and Ambrose. How can people get that bent out of shape over some dumb article written by an obvious idiot?"

"They were that mad, huh?"

"The well-known duo of Eastland and Gilmore hasn't been nominated for the Most Popular Jocks of the Year Award," he informed me.

On Sunday I planted myself in front of the TV with Max in my lap and watched football with Dad and Logan, hardly paying attention to the games. I scarfed down potato chips, cookies, and ice cream and washed it all down with soda in steely revolt of my new plans to become a health food junkie and add more lean muscle mass. By nighttime, I didn't know which was hurting more—my head or my stomach. I dreaded Monday morning. The day of reckoning. When I finally fell asleep, I was so beat that I never heard my alarm clock go off the next morning. Only when Mom tapped on my door did I realize that I had missed the Monday morning meeting of "The Power of Understanding."

25

Walking into the front lobby, I found Cam surrounded by team members. A few of them were holding newspapers. Nancy and Ashley were there, too. Several sets of eyes turned toward me and then looked away. Nobody spoke. It was almost like I wasn't even there.

Melvin Barr, who had been one of the first to take up for me at practices, came in the door behind me and passed me without a word. He was a talented fullback and his dad sometimes volunteered at practices. Both of them had set their hearts on a college football scholarship for Mel.

"Hey, Mel!" I put up a hand, but he never turned back.

Standing there with my hand still in air, I felt my face burning. Matt sneered at me, and I stuck my hand in my pocket. He jerked his chin, pointing it toward the stairs like he wanted me to see something.

What I saw turned my stomach to ice water.

Sam was standing on the stairway with Brady. As I stared at them, Brady put his hand out and dropped it on her shoulder.

I snapped my head away and heard a few snorts of laughter.

"Aww," Matt said. "Somebody took Sticky Fingers's girlfriend."

Sam *wasn't* my girlfriend. But if not, then why did it hurt so much?

Tony came in, ignored the glares from Cam and his crowd, and stopped beside me. "Going my way?"

I nodded, looking at the wall as we passed Sam and Brady on the stairs. "You save the paper?" I asked.

"My mom's got it on the refrigerator with the part about me in yellow highlights. From the looks of Cam and his toadies, you'd think we wrote the damn thing. Up theirs!"

I envied him his anger. It was definitely an improvement on my own misery.

"Hang in there," he said, heading toward his homeroom.

I walked into mine, dropped into a seat, and started working on half-done homework. Sam came in, took the desk beside mine, and started poring through a notebook.

"Hi," I said, avoiding her eyes.

She pretended not to hear me, but finally glanced up, sighed, and looked at me reproachfully. "How could you, Joey?"

"I slept through the alarm."

Her first impulse to lecture me immediately turned to worry. "What do you think Mrs. C. will do?" she murmured anxiously.

"I'd like my remains to be donated to Perry's biology project."

She almost smiled. "I knew you'd be avoiding me. That was why you walked right past me on the stairs, wasn't it?"

"Not exactly," I mumbled. I felt uncool saying it, but I was used to shooting straight with Sam. "It was more that—well, you were with Brady. I didn't want to interrupt."

Her eyes opened wide. "You thought I was with Brady?"

"You weren't?"

She reached out a hand and touched mine briefly. A tiny smile was on her lips. "It was more that he was with me. I told him I had some work to do and had to get to homeroom."

"He isn't good enough for you, Sam."

"You really think so?" Her smile widened. "Listen, if you apologize to Mrs. C., I know she'll forgive you, Joey. She's so wonderful."

"And scary," I added as the bell dinged.

"Yeah, that, too. See you in Reading and Language. I've got to find Alice. We're doing a report together." She hurried out. I stood up, putting my statistics book away. A hand tapped me on the shoulder.

When I turned around, Ashley was standing there. Nancy was with her, but she passed us without a word, glaring at Ashley. "Nancy's mad," Ashley explained. "Because of what the writer said about Cam. She wants to be married to a famous quarterback. She's afraid college coaches won't want him now."

"*I* didn't write that stuff."

"I know that, Joey," Ashley said with a sweet smile. "But it doesn't stop everybody else having sour grapes. Except me," she added. "I don't have any sour grapes at all.

I think you're a wonderful wide receiver." She seemed to be waiting for me to say something.

It was the perfect time to ask her out. Yet I gawked at her without saying a word.

Finally she turned toward the door. "See you later, okay?"

"Okay." Watching her leave, I wondered why I hadn't grabbed the moment. Why hadn't I spoken up? Even stranger, why was I still thinking about Brady's hand on Sam's shoulder?

26

Tombstone spent most of biology glaring at me, this time over the dissection slab. Today we were extracting DNA using real rats, instead of virtual dissection.

"What's your problem?" I asked.

"*You're* my problem," he told me, making an expert incision. "I get nothing from you. Your attention is not on your work and you don't have the intelligence I'd hoped for when I chose you. You're just a meat-headed football player."

A buzzing started to fill my ears and my scalpel shook in my hand. He quickly pushed it away from the slab, not wanting my nervous breakdown to spoil his rat-shaped masterpiece. It didn't help that I felt horribly sorry for the rat.

"Get off my case, Tombstone," I said shortly.

"Don't call me that. Is being a jerk part of playing football?"

"Is making other people feel like idiots part of being a genius?"

He shrugged. "I never thought you were an idiot before.

But how do you think it feels to have a partner who doesn't do his work?"

"How do you think it makes me feel to have to dissect this poor rat when I'd rather dissect your brain?"

He sighed and made another perfect cut, exposing the rat's brain. "Just enjoy your A in dissection today, Eastland. If the rest of your schoolwork's anything like what you're doing in this class, your report card will be a disaster. That's my only comfort."

I gritted my teeth and dug holes into his eyes with my own. You would never expect a smart aleck like Perry to have soft, brown button eyes. They could have belonged to a puppy. If I hadn't suddenly pictured myself pinned to the slab and Perry slicing into me, exposing all the parts in me that hurt the worst, maybe I would have told him I'd made my DNA collections and we could call for our appointment at Bioscope. Instead I took a step forward until our faces were only inches apart. His nose looked to have sprung goose bumps.

"Just curious about something," I hissed between my teeth. "Exactly what do you get out of being such a miserable little butthead? You do realize, I suppose, that you make people feel like flattening you?"

"Like you?"

"Yeah, like me. Right now I feel like pulverizing you."

"I can take care of myself, don't you worry. Back up, you're crowding me."

"Why don't *you* back up?"

Our voices had risen without either of us realizing it.

"A bad dissection isn't worth a fight," Mr. Adams said

from several tables away. "It also isn't worth bringing both your grades down an entire letter grade. Now *I'm* saying it. Back up, and I mean back up."

We backed up, still glaring at each other. Fighting Perry would be like fighting a cooked noodle. Unless he was a black belt in some kind of martial arts that could make him twirl like a whirling dervish, he wouldn't have a chance.

"Okay, what happened to your rat?" Mr. Adams asked, coming briskly to our table and peering down at our slab. He looked closer, obviously surprised. "It looks very good. I thought one of you had gone up the wrong end."

It was supposed to be a joke, but I didn't laugh at dead animal jokes. Perry, on the other hand, chuckled nervously in a falsetto voice.

The A we both got made us even more furious. Him, because he had done most of the work. Me, because he bragged about it to the tables on both sides of us. I had never wanted anything more in my life than I wanted now to bash him. Maybe Cam and Matt would even like me better once I made a shrimp salad out of the whining little dork.

They might like me better still if I got suspended from school and thrown off the team. Stupid idea. But it played on my mind like the image of that helpless little rat pinned to the dissecting block with Perry's knife probing around inside its brain.

As if my day wasn't already bad enough, right after biology I bumped into Mrs. Cunningham in the hallway. "I want to talk with you, Mr. Eastland," she said, jabbing a red fingernail at me like a bloody ice pick. "*Now!* Before my class starts!"

Judging from her face, she wasn't calling me in to congratulate me on Friday night's game. The way she walked in front of me down the hall, scarf flying and heels clicking, you'd have thought she was marching to Armageddon.

I had no choice but to march along behind her to the room. She closed her door behind us, instructing the rest of her curious students to wait outside. Then she went to her desk. I stood in front of it.

"Tell me," she said, her face expressionless. "Tell me why I left my bed more than an hour early this morning to meet with four other students, while you could not be bothered to attend."

I wished desperately that I could explain there had been a horrible accident. I had slipped in the shower. Or I had choked on my breakfast and would have died, save for an emergency tracheotomy.

Sighing, I said, "I didn't hear the alarm."

"Pardon me?"

"I overslept."

"I see. And that's supposed to be a good reason for missing your meeting this morning? You had all weekend to rest up from your triumph on Friday night, Eastland."

Even her eyebrows were glaring at me. "You made an agreement with me to be accountable to our project," she said. "I happen to take accountability very personally. You see, just between the two of us, I came from a family where *nobody* was accountable. Not my mama and not my daddy. I could have gone down the tubes, Eastland. Going down the tubes is easy. You just sit on the top of the slide and let go."

"You think I'm going down the tubes?"

"*You* don't think you are?" she asked. "I present to you two examples. One, you stood up your entire project team. Then there is *this!*" She peeled a paper from her desk and handed it to me.

It was my paper on *I Know Why the Caged Bird Sings*. There was a big ugly red F on it. I stared at it in fascination, never having seen such a thing on one of my papers.

"Never," Mrs. C. said, her voice shaking with anger, "did I expect to see this caliber of work from you. You have never before handed me a paper that wasn't written in perfect grammar, footnoted, beautifully researched, and carefully thought out. This one is without a single redeeming feature. What can you possibly say for yourself that would excuse this?"

I opened my mouth, quaking at the thought of the two-paged, double-spaced paper I would be handing in today, and stood speechless.

"And this better have *nothin'* to do with football," she snapped. "I don't even want to hear that *word* from you."

The bell dinged and someone opened her door a crack.

"Five minutes," she said without turning to look. The door closed. "Go ahead, Eastland. I'm waiting."

"Indirectly, it has something to do with . . . that," I said, "but not exactly."

Her icy stare would have been great at getting criminals to confess to crimes. Sure enough, pretty soon I was spilling out my guts to her. I told her about how nobody had liked me when I first made the team. But a little at a time, they'd started to accept me.

"Then something happened." I tried to go on, but a bull-frog was sitting on my Adam's apple.

"The article," she said without missing a beat.

I should have known she'd read it. She seemed to know everything.

"And just the second I was almost in—I was out." I sounded so pathetic to my own ears, I thought she'd get tears in her eyes and say she understood.

Her eyes stayed bone dry.

"Do you think . . . could I . . . that is, my paper . . ."

"Will stay an F." She grabbed it back from me, put it on top of a stack of other papers, and leaned across the desk. "And no, you won't be getting an A in English from me this term. This whole ugly mess is what is called a consequence. And if your work isn't superb from here on out, it will get even worse."

Until this moment, I hadn't really put a lot of value on my grades, but all at once the loss of my perfect record stabbed me in the gut. "The . . . the paper due today." I could hardly talk. "C-could I have another day or . . .?"

"My grades aren't favors, Eastland. They are earned. You will turn in your paper on time like the others. And don't go missing any more project meetings!"

"Yes ma'am."

She rose from her chair and strode to the door. As she opened it, she looked back at me. "Congratulations on your success in football. If your work improves, I'll let you start saying the name of your sport again."

"Thanks," I said dully.

Her students charged into the room, and Mrs. C.

smiled. "Come in, come in! I'm so sorry to have kept you waiting."

Sam sat beside me and looked at me anxiously. "You okay?"

"Yeah, sure," I lied as I dug my lousy paper out of my notebook, imagining another red F on top of it. Now a D would be the very best I could hope for this semester. Knowing Mrs. C., an F was more likely.

It rained all week, a deluge that cancelled our practices, making us resort to working out in the gym and listening to tactical talks in front of a blackboard. There was no biking home with Tony. Dad left his sales clerk in charge of the store and dropped us both at our separate homes to study.

The week dragged by with U.S. history dates mixing together in my head and French no longer a breeze. My geometry test seemed surprisingly hard. Statistics was even worse. Why had I picked such a challenging elective? I began to review *The Color Purple* in preparation for my next paper, empathizing with Celie, the leading character, who served as the world's punching bag. Then I put it aside, too depressed to continue. But in biology I began to excel, grimly determined to keep up with Perry Toomey.

27

"Whatever you do," Cam said furiously before Friday night's away game, "stop the showboating. You're making me and the whole team look bad."

I obliged him by being lousy. The rest of the team had the foul luck of being even worse. Our offense was zapped and paranoid. Cam was sacked four times and threw for eight yards. Melvin was so eager to show his talent that he drew one penalty after the other and ended up in negative yardage. Brady missed two field goals, and the defense allowed the worst offense in the district to march down the field for two touchdowns. The Bulldogs had lost their winning ways.

Tony played for all of us. Without a team behind him, he still managed to get a ball five yards from the Gibbs Meadows' end zone, and Brady finally got one over.

When the whistle blew at halftime, I found myself facedown in the mud with the ball in front of me. Overhead the scoreboard read: Visitors 3, Home 14.

No hand reached down to pull me to my feet. Nobody said a word as I dragged myself off the ground. I ran to catch up to Tony, but he looked at me angrily and turned away.

"What do you want from me?" I mumbled.

"The same thing I want from myself," he snapped. "Your best." He walked ahead of me without a backward glance.

Coach Miller's face was washed out and grim under the locker room's overhead lights. "Notes aren't going to do squat," he said. "Whatever's happening out there has nothing to do with notes." He laid down his clipboard and looked at us. "We're a team. We don't let people talk into our game. We don't let some damn sportswriter take away our pride, not as a team and not as individuals." He looked at me. "We don't play down. Go on back out there and show me what you're made of. And remember, play as a team. Power lies in unity."

But this time words didn't cut it. We lost the game to an inferior team, 31-10, our first loss since I became a Bulldog. If there was any good news, it was that it wasn't a conference game, so it didn't count toward the regional playoffs.

The drunk was there again and showed even more class tonight by throwing a full trashcan over the fence and onto the field. As before, security took the jerk away. Though actually I thought he had made a good point.

I didn't go out to eat after the game. My fingers were slipping on the edge of the slide. I was going downhill faster and faster.

To make it worse, Brady turned into Sam's shadow. He stared at her in homeroom and walked her to class. Once I saw him slipping a card through the slots of her locker. I knew I shouldn't care. But my stomach felt hollow.

By Wednesday, Brady was sitting next to her in homeroom. I ignored them both and moved closer to Ashley, who still seemed friendly, only maybe not quite so much as she had, say, a week ago. Before my last game.

"Were you sick last week?" she murmured. "In the game, I mean."

"Oh. Right, the game. Yeah, a little. Touch of stomach flu." I wondered uncomfortably if, on top of everything else, I was now turning into a chronic liar.

She brightened a little. "Luckily it wasn't an important game. You're okay now, right?"

"Right."

I found her waiting for me in front of Reading and Language Arts. "Why don't we sit together?" She smiled.

Looking across the hall where Brady had cornered Sam against a locker, I nodded. "Great."

After the last bell I found Sam standing at the side exit door leading to the locker room. Her arms were crossed and she looked both furious and hurt. I needed to get changed, but I stood there staring at her with my mouth open.

As usual she got straight to the point. "Why have you been avoiding me?"

"I haven't been—"

"Yes, you have, Joey. The only time we've talked in the last few days is when I've come up to you. You don't even sit next to me in classes anymore."

I stalled, feeling my face redden. "I thought . . . you and Brady . . ."

Now *her* face went red. "Me and *Brady*?" She looked

suddenly happier. "Well, um, I guess he has been hanging around me some. But that shouldn't bother you, right? Since we're just friends?"

"Oh no," I said quickly. "It doesn't bother me at all."

Her smile faded. "Just like it doesn't bother me at all that you're hanging around Blondie."

"It doesn't?"

She shook her head at me and sighed. "Honestly, Joey, for someone so smart, you can be the biggest idiot."

Before I could say anything, she turned and almost flew down the hallway, leaving me more confused than ever. Dazed, I headed for the locker room. Our next game was at home with Sugar Creek, last year's regional champs. If we lost, we would probably be out of contention for playoffs.

But in our first practice of the week, I looked into Cam's cold eyes and once again played less than my best.

28

Before we headed onto the field on game night, Tony waved me over. He didn't pull any punches. "You gonna play out there tonight or lay down?" he asked bluntly.

"Lay down?" I repeated indignantly. "I've never laid down—"

"Like a blanket on a beach," he returned. "Last Friday and every practice since. And you know it."

I looked at the floor.

"You think this crew will take you back if you play like dung?" he asked. "They'd love for you to look bad. By the way, I heard there was a state scout in the stands last week. How does that make you feel?"

I looked at him sickly. A scout from the state university. And I'd played almost as badly as when I'd first tried out for the team.

"Tony, wait. I'll do better." I was talking to his back.

He turned around. "I hope so, Joey. I really do. If you're trying to make friends with the snobs, you won't do it by making a fool of yourself. That group only takes winners."

Standing there feeling shaky, I felt the Great Receiver suddenly tap me on the shoulder.

The kid makes a good point, he said.

Yeah. He did.

We lined up, and I heard a cheer building outside. It was game time.

I snapped my helmet on, lowered my head, and charged from the locker room with the others.

Coin toss. Cam's magical powers failed him and we had to kick to the Sugar Creek Bears.

The Bears were savvy, well trained, and seasoned. Their team had been to the Division II playoffs every year in the last five, capturing two championships. They had four all-star players: their quarterback, their center, a linebacker, and a free safety. They were also undefeated this season.

We kicked to them and they returned thirty yards.

"First play," Tony said beside me on the bench. "And they're already on the move."

It got worse quick. In only three passes, they scored a touchdown, followed by an extra point.

As our kickoff return team took the field, the coach called me aside and looked me in the eye. "You remember I once told you that a wide receiver finds out what he's made of over the middle?"

I nodded.

"That's true. But you also find out what you're made of when you're playing two teams—theirs and yours. You have to give your team all the loyalty and respect they aren't giving you, Eastland, or we're all lost. But if you can do it, you'll be a receiver to be reckoned with. Understand?"

Blinking back at him, I felt someone stir inside of me, and I knew the GR was with me tonight. He was stronger than me, better than me. And he still loved the team I was starting to hate.

It was he that answered, "Yeah, Coach. I'll give you all I've got."

"Good enough! Have a great game!" He slapped me on the back, and I went running onto the field.

We started with a running play, getting short yardage up the center with Melvin Barr handling the ball. The next play was a pass.

Be smart, the GR whispered. *Eyes on the ball. Quick cuts. No fumbles.*

It was a medium pass, about fifteen yards, and right on the money. Cam might not like me, but his arm did. He put the ball right in my hands, and I turned midstride and streaked downfield.

All the way. Outrunning both safeties, I streaked into the end zone. The screams of the crowd told me I had just made the most spectacular TD of my short career.

Tony ran behind me to the bench and grabbed me by the shoulder. "You're back! Good job!"

Nothing could stop me after that. I caught balls like I was catching live hand grenades and couldn't afford to let one hit the ground. Cam's frowns had lost their hold on me tonight. It was the Great Receiver, not me, out there playing.

I was only dimly aware of time passing, or even the score. Though I knew we were ahead, I also knew that Sugar Creek was close and capable at any moment of changing the tide. I concentrated on separating every play into a universe of its own, giving all I had in whatever way I could. I threw my whole body into my blocks, extended my legs into their longest stride. I ignored charging linebackers and made the crunch receptions.

The hydration therapists and Karen Harris crowded around me on the sidelines with congratulations and so much water I couldn't drink it all. There was a bond between us. Maybe, I thought, more so than with some of the team.

At halftime, I heard a few encouraging words from Melvin, Brian, and some of the others. But there was not a word from Cam. His eyes were chips of ice.

In the locker room, the coach gave me no corrections. He only looked at me and nodded. "You're in the zone, Eastland. Stay there."

In the third quarter, we had two key defensive players go out with minor injuries, and the Bears came back to tie. We hung there for the rest of the quarter and into the fourth, when the Bears took the lead with a long field goal.

Our bench looked like it got the breath kicked out of it. Every sweat-streaked face was hurting.

The GR got in my face. *Don't think about the score. That's none of your business. Think about mechanics. Keep your heart. Keep your courage and your good hands. Run your routes. Keep doing your best.*

With a minute to go on the clock and still down by three, Cam threw a twenty-yard bullet, way too high and seemingly beyond my reach.

I jumped, my right arm stretching to its last inch.

The ball stuck to my right palm. I caught up to it with the left and brought it down, already in stride. The Bears came at me from all directions, but I muscled through the last linebacker and charged toward the end zone.

Pride raged in me suddenly and went straight to my head. I was the best. Go suck on this, turncoats!

Inches from the goal line, I flew faster, holding up the ball in one-handed triumph. And a charging Bear punched it out.

I grabbed for the football—too late—even as the speaker overhead roared, "*Fumble, fumble!*"

At least half a dozen players from both teams threw themselves toward the ball.

I dived desperately into the pack, taking a fist in the face and a kick in the groin. But when the referee cleared the mound off me, I had the football, hanging on with both hands.

Red-faced, I ran back to the huddle. It was deadly silent. We had time for only one play. We could kick for a tie or try for the win.

No one looked at me. I felt myself trembling. That close and I had bobbled the ball. Doing just what they had accused me of: showboating.

"Pay attention, hotdog," Cam said contemptuously.

I nodded, keeping my eyes on the ground.

The coach called a running play. With only inches to go, Melvin would try to muscle the ball into the end zone. The ball was snapped and Cam shuffled it cleanly into Mel's hands. The Bears were ready for it; there was nowhere to run. Mel cut right and headed toward the sideline, where I was a decoy. Only one problem—the corner-back guarding me read the play and headed off on a beeline toward Mel. He was undersized but a speedster. No way was Mel going to outrun him. I streaked after him, and Mel saw me and strung out the play by running laterally toward me and turning the charging CB in my direction. I was between them now and got into a blocking stance. The corner ran right over me, knocking me on my butt and grabbing Mel.

Mel dug in, dragged him two steps, then dived over the goal line. We had won the game.

In the locker room, Cam made it clear just who had been responsible for the win: Melvin. "After Eastland blew it, you saved it, Mel!" he said defiantly.

There were rumbles of agreement from the usual circle around him, but Melvin held out his hand and grasped mine. "Thanks for running interference," he said gruffly. "You don't take that hard block for me and we don't win."

"Yeah, some block, getting creamed by a midget cornerback," Roddy Dugan sneered. "Not to mention he'd already almost lost the game by another bonehead showboat."

Coach Miller came in the locker room, followed by Coaches Stanley and Brewster, just in time to hear his words. Roddy backed up and fell over a bench.

None of the team said a word as he righted himself and sat. Every face had gone tense.

Coming through the door, the Coach had looked younger, joyful, and full of the same kind of fire he must have had in his glory days in high school and college. But in only seconds, he had gained about twenty years and lost his spark.

He nodded around the room. "Our biggest win in over ten years against what some believe to be the best team in the district. A game that puts us into heavy contention for the playoffs. And I walk into this."

Roddy paled as the Coach turned directly to him. "Don't let me interrupt you, Doogan. You were saying?"

After a long pause, Roddy muttered rebelliously, "Well, he is a showboat."

"Is he?" the Coach said thoughtfully. "Still can't get that article out of your mind, can you? Joey didn't write it, in case you—"

But to my own surprise I was standing, my larynx so strained I could hardly speak. "Coach?"

He looked at me. "Do you want to answer him, son?"

"Yes sir. The truth is, he's right. I almost lost us the game."

For the first time Coach Miller smiled. "Well said. Yes, Eastland, you came as close to losing a game you helped us win as anything I've ever seen. Too many games are lost like that, rubbing the ball up somebody's craw. But I must say . . ." The Iron Jaw looked fiercely into every listening face in the room before he went on. "If I'd been in your position, I'm not sure I wouldn't have done the same. A face gets tired of being spit in. Anybody ever think about that? Or like I was beginning to say before Eastland interrupted me, did it occur to anybody here that he didn't write that damn article?"

Roddy's face was redder than before I took the heat for him. He shook his head, but didn't answer.

Neither did anyone else.

"Does anybody know who that sportswriter is?" Coach went on.

More heads shook.

"I asked Jim Gardiner, who usually writes that column in the *Sentinel*, because the language was pretty unfriendly. Nasty even. You might say it was almost designed to rip our team apart. And that is exactly what happened.

"Turns out the man who wrote it is a visiting ex-athlete who's now a sportswriter for a big paper in New York. His nephew was playing on the team we beat that night, and he approached Jim and asked to cover the game. As a courtesy, Jim felt obliged to honor the request. I would have explained this earlier, but he just told me about it and offered his apologies." He looked at Cam. "How does it feel to let some hotshot reporter make chump-meat out of you? Destroy your team, just like he'd bragged he would? He was stuck with the fact that we won; he couldn't deny it. So he used one of the oldest tricks in the book. He picked out two key players and damned the rest. And you all fell for it."

Fiery red, Cam stammered, "B-but he talked about how Tony was his favorite player!"

"He'd never seen him play before in his life. He read a few articles and winged it."

Almost every head in the locker room was down, nobody willing to meet the coach's eyes. The room was silent. Nobody moved.

Then in the stillness Tony's voice rang out. "Oh well, I guess I can tell my mom to take that article off the refrigerator."

Every face turned to look at him. There was a long pause. Then suddenly the room rocked with laughter. Coaches and players roared.

I put my arm on Tony's back. I couldn't say anything; there was a lump in my throat.

Later at the Chocolate Shoppe, I sat with Sam, Alice, and Tony and looked around the room.

"What's on your mind, Joey?" Tony asked.

"Well, we're a team again, but nothing has really changed. I mean . . ." I couldn't explain. I looked over at Cam. He and his usual friends had cornered one area. After all we'd been through together these last weeks, my status with Cam and his group hadn't changed in the least.

And once again, people I had considered to be members of the loop were scattered about the room, not even looking Cam's way. Could the group I'd admired for so long be just Cam and his inner circle? Maybe our student body couldn't be so easily divided into the "ins" and the "outs." There were probably a lot of groups. And those groups no doubt mixed together and made still more groups. It was confusing.

Sam squeezed my hand under the table and whispered, "I notice you haven't asked Blondie out yet."

"I've haven't seen you dating Brady either."

"Could it be that maybe we're dating each other and you just haven't noticed yet?"

I grinned at her slowly. "I think I noticed," I said, squeezing her hand back. The truth was, I hadn't even noticed if Ashley was in the room.

Holding Max cradled against my chest, I tried to let myself into the dark bedroom without making a sound. Logan hadn't gone to the game and had no doubt been asleep for hours. The SATs were tomorrow morning.

I crept past him and carried Max up the ladder, hoping it wouldn't creak.

"How'd it go?" Logan asked suddenly. He sounded alert and wide awake.

I crawled onto my bed and settled Max. Then I lay on my belly, my head hanging down over the side of the bed, the way Logan and I had talked for years.

"We won."

"Great." He smiled up at me, his head lying on his crossed arms. "Were you good?"

"Some good stuff. One horrible play that almost lost the game for us."

"Then you were great," my brother assured me. "I'd sure settle for having only one horrible answer tomorrow."

"You've got a better perspective than me." I eased into a better position, every muscle and bone throbbing. "What are you doing still awake?"

"Studying. Mary Pat rigged me up with earphones."

"If you don't get some sleep, you won't remember anything tomorrow."

He plucked the earphones from his ears and threw

them on the floor. "You're right. I'm just a little worried."

"You'll do fine, Logan. You're one of the smartest people I know."

"Thanks, Joey," he said in a muffled voice. "Well, good night then."

When I closed my eyes, football never even crossed my mind. I just lay there hoping that my brother could ace his test tomorrow.

29

The next morning, Logan got up early and studied right through breakfast. Then the doorbell rang. All of a sudden I saw the pulse hammering in his throat.

"It's Mary Pat," Mom hollered from the other room. "I'll get it."

"She's early," Logan mumbled. He gulped down some juice just as she barreled in, wearing high-heeled boots that made her at least three inches taller.

She was dressed all in black, like she was on her way to a funeral.

"Terrific game last night, Joey." She smiled at me. "Even if you almost blew it there at the end."

"Thanks."

She turned on Logan. "Are you *centered?*" She sighed. "No, you look about as centered as the nose on your face."

Logan's face was gray. "My nose is out of line?"

"Never mind. *Breathe*, or you're going to keel over." She hung over the back of his chair.

Logan stared up at her. Or rather, he stared at her neck. He couldn't seem to take his eyes off it.

It did look a little like an anaconda.

"Come *on*, honey, we've got to get crackin'." She ran her fingers through his hair, trying to straighten out the cowlicks. "We can study in the car and I'll give you last-minute pointers."

Logan stayed where he was.

"What's wrong with you?" Mary Pat frowned.

Logan said nothing. Loudly.

Mary Pat sighed, then reached in her purse for her pad and pen.

Oh, no, I thought. *She's going to draw him again.*

Sure enough, she started sketching. So far we'd seen her draw a pinhead on a ball of mush; Logan lost in a band formation with his hat slipped down over his nose; Logan in a shirt she didn't like; Logan trying to drive a car with a head that was shorter than the steering wheel; Logan with ice cream smeared over his mouth.

We sat frozen, waiting for the latest horror to find its way onto Mary Pat's sketch pad.

"Here you go, honey," she said sweetly, handing the open pad to him. "This is the way you look this morning."

He looked at it silently. It was a doozy. There was Logan in midflight, every hair on his head sticking out like gummed-up bird tails. Juice drooled down his chin. His sweater was half tucked in, half out. Pens, pencils, and erasers flew everywhere as he ran across the page.

"Where am I supposed to be running?" he asked in a flat emotionless voice.

"Let's hope it's not to yet another failure. Come on, let's get it over with. Remember, I'm with you no matter how badly you do."

Logan suddenly sat up straight and ripped the pen out of her hand. He looked ready to break it in half.

"What are you doing, Logan?" Mary Pat asked nervously.

Logan flipped to a fresh page in her pad and pushed the pen's point into the page hard enough to stab out an eye. A crazy smile crossed his face. "What if I draw a picture of *you*?" he said, sketching a bloated face with a mouth the size of the Grand Canyon.

She looked stunned. "I look like that?"

"A little," my brother said, sketching a noticeable tummy. "You've gained weight lately, you know. All those shakes and fries, I guess. But then I'm not very good at drawing proportions. Small brain and all."

"I am not fat!" she said furiously.

"You are certainly not skinny," Logan retorted. "In fact, of the two of us, I'm closer to the right weight."

Her face turned beet-red and she clutched her sweater around her, trying to hide her stomach. "Logan," she said, "we don't have time for this. I need every second to prepare you."

"I don't think so, Mary Pat," he said. "I don't need any more help from you. You can go on home now."

He tucked the pad back into her purse and then took a hearty bite of breakfast.

"Don't be like that." She was shaking. Her voice

choked up; tears filled her eyes. "You . . . you don't have a chance without me."

"Ah, well," he said.

"Logan, please. *Please!*"

But for once my brother did not give in. He took a huge bite of toast and scrambled eggs and walked her to the door, chewing. I trailed after him, forgetting this was none of my business.

"Bye now," he said to her.

"Logan, don't do this!" She grabbed his arm.

I'd never seen Mary Pat cry before, but she did it as well as she did everything else. Full out. It did her no good at all. In a matter of seconds, she found herself outside the door.

"Sorry to make this short," Logan said. He still had a piece of toast in his hand. He took another bite and mumbled, "I have a test to take. Don't worry, I'm prepared to live with whatever score I get." He closed the door and locked it, leaving Mary Pat outside, howling. Then he headed back to the kitchen, looking more cheerful than he had in months. He even looked a couple of inches taller.

Mom had just come down, P.S. scooting down the steps on his bottom behind her, *thump, thump, thump.* She stood there with her mouth open, staring back and forth between the closed door and the kitchen.

"What's that sound?" she said, listening hard, her eyebrows bunched up.

"It's Mary Pat," I said.

"No, not that."

"I don't hear anything else—" I began. But then I did. It was a tuneless sort of hissing noise that had Max shooting toward the stairs, whining desperately. It sounded like a broken teapot.

"It's Logan," Mom said, wide-eyed. "He's . . . whistling."

The two of us looked at each other in wonder. Logan whistling on SAT morning!

30

"Don't let it get out," Cam said, "but we're holding a kind of party in the park on Saturday at about two."

It was Thursday night. I stood there holding the phone, wondering if it was really Cam on the other end or a joke. "Uh, why shouldn't I let it get out?" I expected to hear a big guffaw on the other end.

"It's more or less a team party, but a lot of kids won't be invited," Cam explained. "Also it's no-crows-or-jumping-beans, just so you understand. You know what I'm talking about, right?"

"Right," I said. I didn't have a clue what he meant.

"Good. We're meeting where they have Shakespeare in the summer. There's a platform there."

"You mean outside in the park? It's going to be about thirty degrees."

"We're hardy, right?"

"Right, but—"

"See you there."

Tony was watching from the floor, having a tug of war with both dogs at once. "What's up?"

"Do you know about Cam's party in the park?"

He hesitated and suddenly dropped the cord he was holding, both surprised dogs flying backward.

"Well, no, actually I didn't hear about it," he said slowly. "Isn't it a little cold for outdoor parties?"

"I thought that, too. It doesn't make sense, does it?"

"No. Did he say anything else?"

Despite my best intentions, my old crazy dream of being part of Cam's group came back, and I started to get excited. "Just something about no crows or jumping beans. Do you know what that means?"

"Yeah, Joey, I do. I certainly do understand what Cam is telling you." He sighed. "I knew you'd find out sooner or later."

"Tony, what are you talking about?"

"Well, for instance, crows." He stopped.

"Yeah?"

"A crow would be me. Or Melvin. Or Ed Bent." He looked at me intently.

My stomach dropped. "Tony," I said hoarsely, "you don't mean . . . *black*? Are you saying Cam doesn't invite blacks to his parties?"

"That's exactly what I'm saying, and he doesn't invite jumping beans either. That's the cute little name he came up with for Latinos. Since the 'N word' isn't much tolerated anymore, or any other loaded monikers, he's come up with his own words. He and his set can use them right in the halls and the teachers don't understand what they're saying. I guess he figured you'd probably heard about it."

"I knew he wasn't the nicest guy. I didn't know he was a racist."

"I think Cam's more an elitist than anything else. He doesn't like certain ethnic groups or the poor or the uncool or girls who are a few pounds overweight. He senses when people are shy and goads them. Like he used to do with you."

I collapsed to the floor beside him, feeling so sick that I couldn't imagine ever catching another ball from Cam or even walking onto the same field with him.

"So what time's the party?" he asked.

"Two o'clock. I wouldn't go if you held a gun to my head. Or . . . wait a minute." I hesitated, having been hit with an idea. "I mean I wouldn't go unless—"

"Unless what?"

I grinned at him. "What say we go together? And why don't we get Melvin and Ed and José and Ricardo and Ambrose, and all the other guys who aren't usually included? Why don't we all show up at the party together? They can slam a door in our faces, but the park's open to everybody."

"Might be a dangerous move."

"For them, you mean," I said. "You think that bunch wants to take on Ambrose and José and Ricardo and Diego Silva? What about Ed? He's not only tall, he's a crusher. Have you noticed his biceps? Listen, Tony, I am personally inviting you to Cam's party!"

Tony didn't move or speak for a few minutes. Then suddenly he started laughing. "You're on, Joey. I accept your invitation. But there's one thing I don't understand. What are they up to on Saturday afternoon in the park? There's something rotten about this; I can feel it. It's not going to be your regular party, you can bet your jersey on that!"

Logan wandered listlessly into the room. "Who's going to a party?"

"We are," I said. "You wanna go?"

"Who, me? I'm not going anywhere until I hear the results of that test. I'm sure I loused up the mechanical section. I knew I should have spent more time on graphics and model engineering." Logan collapsed on the couch with his iPod. "I thought the critical reading section was pretty good. But statistics . . ." He groaned.

"Speaking of tests," Tony said to me, "how did you do in your finals? Report cards come out next week, you know."

"I think I pulled out As in biology and French and at least Bs in history and geometry. I'm not sure about statistics. But my reading and language arts will probably be a D. Or even worse." I saw Tony wince. "I'll just have to bring it up next semester. Sam will be on my case about it."

Tony nodded. "You guys want to go to a movie on Saturday night with Alice and me?"

"I think Sam wants to teach me to dance. If you and Alice want to come dance in her basement, we can go to the movie later."

"Great. We'll go to Sam's after our party in the park." He rubbed his hands together in anticipation. "We need to call our guest list now."

"I was wondering: Is Brian Freeman in Cam's group? He doesn't seem like the others."

"Come to think of it, I don't think he is."

"Let's call him, too. How about Brady? He's with that group sometimes, but not all the time, and he kind of hangs in the back." I hesitated.

"He tries to make Cam and his buds think that he's with them and the rest of us think he's not. Mark my words, he'll be skulking around in the background of whatever's happening Saturday."

"You're right. He's out. Let's call the others."

Not one player turned us down.

31

Sam and I met in the school lobby Friday morning before classes began. "What's going on?" Sam pointed at a group gathered around Perry, who was talking excitedly and gesturing with his arms.

"I haven't seen Perry that happy since I've known him," I said.

"Me either. He looks on top of the world."

It wasn't until biology that I found out why. For once Perry wasn't even on my case. All he could talk about was his solar helicopter, finished at last. It could read humidity levels and measure cloud density and wind velocity.

"A patent lawyer heard about it and called me," Perry bragged. "He's going to do all the legal work on it for a 2 percent cut. It's so cool."

"So when are you seeing the lawyer?"

Perry grinned, forgetting to be hostile even though I had not yet given him the go-ahead to call for our appointment at Bioscope Systems. I had been hoping, a little guiltily, to hold off until football season was over. What with practices and games, the international peace project, and catching up with homework, I had no time to spare.

"He's meeting me in the park Saturday afternoon to see a demonstration."

I gaped at him. "Wh-what time?"

"Two o'clock. He'll look at the machine and the plans and decide if he wants to do it. But I know he will!" The bell sounded, and he picked up his backpack.

"Wait, Perry! Where are you meeting?"

"Over by the summer Shakespeare Festival stage. If you want to see the demonstration," he added importantly, "you can come watch. I've invited a lot of people."

"Is your dad coming with you? Or your mom?"

"They're both out of town. Our housekeeper's dropping me off. Don't worry; I'll be fine. No patent lawyer will be able to take advantage of me!"

He was gone before I could close my mouth.

That night's game was with Hudson High School, the last unbeaten team in our division. Before the game I beckoned Tony into a corner of the locker room and told him about Perry's meeting with the patent lawyer.

"Sounds to me like the lawyer is Cam McKey, Esquire, playing a lousy joke," Tony said grimly. "He and Matt have set Saturday as vengeance day on Perry."

"We should warn him. Except what if there really *is* a patent lawyer and Cam plans to sabotage the demonstration?"

"It's possible." Tony frowned. "If Cam's planned something and we report it, the whole team is liable to be suspended, and we'll be out of the playoffs."

"Maybe if we just tell them we know what they're up to, they won't show."

"On the other hand," Tony said rebelliously, "it's about time Cam had to eat a little dirt. He can't pull anything if we're there. I say we show. We've got them out-muscled. And if Perry needs protecting, he's got us!"

"Okay," I agreed, "let's do it that way."

For now we concentrated on the game, where Cam passed for major yardage. In fact it seemed like every other offensive play was Cam to me. On my way back to the bench, I thought about how it had just felt, catching one of his long balls and streaking into the end zone to the cheers of the crowd. After tomorrow we might never be in such sync again. I almost wished he hadn't invited me. Then disgust at my own selfishness set in. No matter what, I was going to the park tomorrow.

Enjoy the night, I thought. Who knows whether you'll ever have another game like this?

It was as good as it could ever get. The offensive line held. Our runners ran in the holes we opened for them. Our defense caused three turnovers and held the second best scoring team in our division to a single touchdown. Brady kicked three field goals, one from forty-two yards, and had four extra points as we routed them 37-7 before putting in our reserves for the final five minutes.

On the surface we were the most connected team to ever take a football field. Underneath the play we were divided into two separate units, set for confrontation in the park tomorrow afternoon.

32

Saturday turned out to be one of the coldest days of the year.

We parked across from the park in four packed vans and watched Cam's group disappear over the hill along with a mass of other kids from school. Obviously Perry had invited a slew of observers to the helicopter demonstration.

"There he is!" Tony hissed.

I looked up to see Perry getting out of a rather drab sedan driven by a woman who must have been his housekeeper. There was a five-year-old version of Perry strapped into a booster seat in the back.

Stealthily we began to unload.

I watched Perry turn toward the open car window. He leaned in, kissed the driver's cheek, and spent a minute talking to her. It was a different Perry than I had ever seen, smiling and *normal*. He tapped on the rear passenger window, waved at his younger brother, and then crossed in front of the car and stood waving them off before heading up the hill.

There were seventeen of us, all from the team, including starters and reserves.

"Let's roll," Tony said, starting off briskly.

Perry looked like an unearthly apparition trudging up the hill in his long black coat and woolen scarf, its ends blowing in the wind. His thin hair swirled about his head; his sharp chin was buried in his scarf. A briefcase hung from his right hand and an awkward and bulky sack swung from his left.

Leading our group were José, Ambrose, and Jackson, the best of our offensive line. Oddly, Cam's only friend among his offensive linemen was Roddy Doogan, the slightest and least talented of those responsible for guarding the quarterback. If he wanted to go pro, he might rethink the wisdom of that.

"Is Sam here?" Tony hissed beside me.

"Of course not, I didn't tell her." I paused, a horrible idea crossing my mind. "Don't tell me you told Alice?"

"Of course I did. She's here."

I frowned, knowing that if Alice was here, then Sam must be, too. How strange, though, that she hadn't called me. Did this mean she approved and hadn't wanted to stop me from coming?

Branches groaned overhead, sending down a shower of damp gold and red leaves. In the distance a dog howled, a long mournful sound.

We reached the top of the hill and followed Perry's long, flapping black coat at a distance, traveling farther into the park toward the Shakespeare Festival stage. It sat in a large clearing overlooking a pond.

We were almost there.

"Close in tighter," Tony commanded.

At his words, the ranks closed around us. I found

myself walking just behind the leaders, Tony on one side of me and Brian on the other, the others on our heels.

"There they are," Brian muttered. "And there's a mob gathered to watch."

Mob was the right word. There had to be more than a hundred people gathered by the stage.

Cam's group stood directly between the stage and Perry and us. He and Matt were in front, of course, and behind them I caught a glimpse of the Doogan brothers, George White, Wayne Yeager, Tommy Brink, and several more Bulldog players, as well as a few popular guys from school. Sure enough, Brady hung at the very back, trying to act as if he had wandered into the action by mistake.

"I don't see any adults," I mumbled, trying to spot a businessman, perhaps holding a briefcase.

"Nope," Tony grunted. "This is definitely a scam. They set a trap for him."

My heart slammed into my ribs as I suddenly spotted Sam in the first row of a large crowd on the far side of the stage, with Alice beside her. Another big crowd was on the near side, and a third, smaller group stood not far from Cam and his crowd. I recognized some of the cheerleaders there, including Ashley and Nancy, all obvious supporters of Cam and Matt.

We were close behind Perry now. He saw Cam and his followers, and spun around to find himself backed up by a weighty honor guard. Beyond them, he found me.

"Joey?" He suddenly looked spooked. "What's going on?"

"We're not your problem, Perry. The problem's over there."

He followed my glance, saw Cam and his followers moving in, and jerked around as though to make a run for it. Then slowly, realizing he was surrounded on both sides, he lifted his chin, turned back, and stood his ground.

I had to admire him. He had to be scared, but was obviously determined to fight the entire bunch, single-handed if need be.

Cam looked coldly past Perry, José, Ambrose, and Jackson to where I stood with Tony and the rest of our group. "I thought you understood, Eastland. But I guess you really don't get it." The look on his face wasn't like his game face. This was real war. This battle was for blood.

I stepped forward and felt Ambrose Morse's large hand close on my shoulder.

"Take it easy. They've got weapons." He nodded toward the weighty hammers in both Cam and Matt's hands. They could do major damage.

"Thanks, Ambrose." I edged forward more slowly and murmured, "Perry, listen. Everybody behind you is with you. You understand? We're on your side."

He looked bewildered and was still searching everywhere, probably still hoping to see the patent lawyer. "Why are there sides? Have you seen the lawyer?"

"I'm sorry, Perry," I said, now standing beside him, "there is no lawyer. It's what this sick bunch would call a joke."

A wave of red crawled up his throat and covered his thin,

sharp-featured face as he looked slowly at Cam and Matt and their gang, and then at the crowds on the sidelines, most of whom he himself had invited to see his triumph.

Cam started toward Perry, Matt beside him. "Stay out of this, Eastland," he warned.

The two of them didn't look the least bit cool to me. They looked ridiculous and ugly as they moved closer to Perry, who was so much smaller than either of them and totally unarmed.

I stepped squarely in front of Perry. "Get back, Cam." He and Matt were only a couple of feet away now, both raising their hammers.

"You were warned," Cam said slowly.

"Yeah. Just know that to get to him, you're going to have to go through me!"

Suddenly Tony was beside me. "And me!"

"And me!" Brian said stoutly, stepping up, too.

Bewildered, Cam then saw his entire offensive line, except for Roddy Doogan, step in front of Tony, Brian, and me. He was now facing José, Ambrose, and Jackson, who had been protecting him all season.

"And me!" the three of them thundered, joined by a chorus of other deep voices: "AND ME!"

Melvin Barr, Ricardo Gonzalez, Ed Bent, and a host of other players followed the defensive line, now closing in hard on Cam and Matt.

Ambrose reached calmly for Cam's hammer. "I'll take that."

Cam had spent too much time under Ambrose's protection not to have respect for his power. He put the hammer into his outstretched hand with only a whimper, shrinking backward into his gang, but Matt had no intention of backing down so easily.

With Ambrose in pursuit, he dove savagely through the unarmed linemen, blasting away with his hammer, fighting his way to the large sack that lay at Perry's feet.

Blood surging, I realized the plan. They meant to destroy Perry's helicopter. Then no doubt, they planned to mock him, humiliate him, and threaten violence if he dared tattle.

Sure enough, Matt reached Perry, smiled tauntingly, and raised his hammer. Perry uttered a piercing, terrified howl and threw himself across the sack.

"You think I care if you get hurt?" Matt put both hands on the handle, raised the hammer higher, and swung down hard.

His hammer never connected with the quivering Perry. Instead he found himself hanging in midair.

Ed Bent had hoisted him as easily as he'd have lifted a sack of garbage. A second later he slammed him to the ground. Diego Silva jerked the hammer from his hand and Melvin, Diego, and Ricardo plopped down on his chest.

He uttered a strangled cry as Ambrose Morse joined the heap. Eyes bugging, gasping for air, Matt flailed around, trying to free himself. No one budged. Breathing raggedly he kicked, bucked, and attempted to roll to one side and then the other, growing more and more panicked.

"This any worse than what you had planned for Perry

Toomey?" Ambrose huffed. He scooted around, making himself more comfortable, finally settling directly over Matt's gut. "Me, I'm feeling real comfy, aren't you?"

A chorus of assents came from the other guys on Matt's chest. They seemed ready to sit there forever, even as Matt kept struggling frantically, straining for every breath.

Pretty soon he was begging.

A couple of Cam's crowd took a few steps forward, then stopped on the spot, hemmed in by muscled linemen and linebackers.

Tony, Brian, and I still stood with Perry, ready to face off any more comers. There was a lull, everybody just standing staring. Then suddenly, it started. The crowd who had come to see Perry fly his helicopter began to cheer.

Perry staggered to his feet, still holding his bag. He looked in disbelief at the kids, stamping their feet and clapping their gloved hands. And then the chanting began.

"What are they saying?" Perry mumbled, looking embarrassed.

I grinned. The crowd was chanting "FLY IT! FLY IT! FLY IT!"

"I think they want to see your machine fly, Perry."

"Wow," he said softly. "I can't believe it!" He stood there, staring at the crowd, speechless for once.

"So? Are we going to see it?"

Smiling widely, he bent to unzip his bag. As he drew out his machine, another huge cheer split the air, growing louder as Perry proudly held up his helicopter, pointing out its precharged solar packs for all to see.

Cam and his bunch tried to sidle off in the uproar, but

their teammates were having none of it. Held captive and red-faced, they were forced to watch Perry's helicopter rise triumphantly in a fury of whirling blades and then soar into the sky.

Sam and Alice joined those of us standing closest to Perry, watching as the helicopter zoomed straight ahead, went up, down, and then performed a bunch of patterns that could have been stolen from the Bulldogs' playbook.

I was so busy watching that I didn't notice Ambrose and his buddies hurriedly scooting off Matt's chest. Matt lay gasping, clutching his gut, and gulping air. Something was happening.

"Over there!" Sam pointed nervously.

Coach Miller, over two hundred pounds of him, was heading toward us at a full-out run. He was hatless, his jacket unzipped, his shirttail out, and his shin-high galoshes unlaced.

"How'd he find out?" Tony muttered.

Sam held up her cell phone. "I called him. We figured he'd have the best chance of breaking this up without getting the team suspended." She looked at me anxiously. "I hope it was the right thing to do."

Tony and I exchanged worried looks.

Coach galloped closer, clutching a stitch in his side.

When he was almost on us I stepped from the pack. "Hey, Coach!" I bellowed.

He did a double take as he saw me and the rest of the team and stopped on the spot, chest heaving.

A few of the players from Cam's group, including Brady, Wayne Yeager, and Tommy Brink, edged away, trying to blend in with the rest of the crowd. Most froze as I stepped forward to meet Coach Miller.

"Eastland?" he grunted, staring at the gathered crowd.

"Everything's okay, sir."

"That a fact?" His face dripped with sweat. He leaned over and put his hands on his knees, trying to get his breath, as he looked warily at Perry. "You okay, too?"

Perry looked from me to Cam. He studied Matt Burris, who still lay panting on the ground. I knew this was the moment. Either Perry would rat or not. If he did, we wouldn't be in the playoffs.

He opened his mouth, and then closed it. He cleared his throat. Still, he said nothing.

Almost reluctantly, Coach stepped closer to Perry. "You have something to tell me, son?"

Perry drew a long breath and hesitated a moment longer. Then his chest rose. His head went up proudly. "No sir," he said loudly, almost defiantly.

The coach studied him more closely. "Nobody tried anything with you?"

"I can take care of myself," Perry replied, stone-faced. His lips closed. He had said all he was going to say.

As a few people started to edge away, word passed through the crowd quickly. And then suddenly scattered cheers started again, rising to a crescendo as more people heard what had happened.

Perry looked around, dazed. "What are they cheering about?" he asked.

I clapped my hand on his shoulder. "You, Perry. They like your style."

He beamed back at me, shaking his head in amazement.

"My lab partner here is doing a model helicopter demonstration," I explained to the coach, pointing at the helicopter that had been making tight little circles overhead since his arrival.

"Yeah," Perry crowed. He manipulated his controls carefully and the helicopter slowed and descended, coming to a perfect landing almost at his feet to the thunderous delight of the crowd.

"You built that?" Coach asked. "Outstanding!"

Perry began to answer, then stopped, as startled as the rest of us when a throng of people headed his way and even the coach had to step back to allow better access to the star of the day. For the time being, Cam, Matt, and the rest of the team was old news.

"I guess the demonstration is over, Coach," I said, seeing he looked both stunned and confused. "You wouldn't want to have an espresso with the team, would you?"

He didn't budge for a few seconds, then he smiled and nodded. "Wouldn't mind." He glanced at Tony, Melvin, and Brian, standing closest to us. "I suppose you can fill me in on what just happened?"

"Well . . ."

"I'll pay," he said. He wiped his forehead with his coat sleeve and motioned the rest of the team toward the hill. "And drive," he added as most of the guys headed for the vans. "I want you four with me."

We left Perry surrounded by a bunch of kids and trudged down the hill in silence.

In the car, the coach looked at the four of us while we

waited for the rest of the guys to climb into the vans. "If you have anything to tell me, now's the time."

For a moment nobody spoke. Tony and Brian examined the scenery.

Then Melvin boomed, "Team business, sir. It rests with us."

The coach's eyebrows rose. "My phone call said Perry Toomey was involved. How did he get mixed up with the team?"

I sighed. "If you knew Perry better, you wouldn't ask, sir. He gets himself mixed up in everything. But I'll say this: He makes a great lab partner. He could dissect you, string out your parts, and put you back together again."

"Sounds like he'd make a good coach," he said. "Well, anybody know a good espresso place? I could use a couple of Danishes, too."

He started the car, then cleared his throat and looked out the window without meeting any of our eyes. "Thanks for whatever you did back there." He took off, leading the line of vans.

I knew he'd never really try to find out exactly what it was.

33

The day before report cards came out, Mrs. C. gave back our last papers.

If there was any way to put a damper on my great mood, it would be seeing another big, fat, red F.

She went round the desks, pausing to have a quiet word with each student, and came to me last. I felt Sam nudge me on the other side, but I still couldn't look Mrs. C. in the eye as she put my paper in front of me. It blurred before my eyes and then suddenly came into focus.

Either I was hallucinating or she had written A+ on the cover page of my theme analysis of *The Heart Is a Lonely Hunter*. I looked up at her blankly. "My paper was so short. . . ."

"Short is not awful, Mr. Eastland. You touched and bruised my heart with your every word. You made me feel the uncertainty, sadness, and separateness of the human condition that existed in each of those lonely characters." She winked. "And your word economy was a big relief from many of the papers I read."

Her robust laugh rang out and she went back to her

desk. I tried to remember how unhappy and separate I'd felt while I was writing that paper.

The day we got our report cards, I saw that Mrs. C. had allowed herself to err on the side of generosity, letting my paper pull me all the way up to a B-. She mentioned "class participation," "homework," and "improvement" in her comments, but I knew what had happened.

Mrs. C. had gone a little soft.

Friday night was our second to last game of the regular season. It was an easy game, a rollover, but Cam's throwing was off. After several bad pass attempts, the coach used the other team's lackluster defense to try out some running plays that we might be able to use in the playoffs.

It was Tony and Melvin's game all the way.

Other teams in contention were taking notes up in the stands. The coach mixed up our plays and tried not to give too many hints.

"Face it, Joey," Sam said later as we sat in the Chocolate Shoppe. "Tony was the star tonight."

"Sad as I am to admit it," I said, winking at Tony, "the kid was not too bad."

The next day, SAT scores were due out. A pale-faced Logan ate no breakfast and stayed in our room, waiting online.

Mom and I hovered in the living room, hoping to hear a triumphant yell. P.S. played on the rug with his cars. Except for his revving sounds there was only silence.

When she couldn't stand the suspense any longer, Mom tiptoed up to our bedroom and cracked open the door. She tiptoed back down. "He's just sitting there, staring at his computer screen," she whispered. "He isn't crying or anything. Or pulling out his hair. Of course, with his hair, it's hard to tell."

P.S. stopped playing and crawled into her lap. He was anxious, too, without really understanding why.

Dad came in for lunch. When Mom suddenly burst into tears and flew into his arms, he looked terrified.

"Was it awful?" he whispered, gray-faced.

"We haven't heard anything yet," she said, still sniffling. "I just wanted to tell you . . ."

"Yeah?" Dad said with trepidation. The awkwardness between them since he'd signed that football release form had not completely disappeared.

She gave him a watery smile. "I love you so much! I love all of you so much. I love our family, and our home, and our animals. And . . . and I just wanted to say . . ." She gulped. "I know that Logan is going to have a high score— a *very high score*—on his SAT!"

Dad closed his arms tighter around her and laid his cheek against her bowed head. "Thank you, Grace."

"You're welcome," she blubbered.

Dad caught my eye over her shoulder and winked. "It'll be all right, dear. Don't forget that our family happens to own its own lucky mascot! How can we lose?"

Heart in my throat, I could only stare at him. After all this time, it had really happened. Max was finally my dog. I blinked hard, but I wasn't the only one with tears in his eyes. Dad's eyes looked a little misty, too, as he added, "At least, our animals are still in single digits!"

He lingered for an extra hour, but eventually he had to go back to work. Mom promised to call him as soon as she knew anything. But he kept calling anyhow.

Mom had barely hung up the phone after his fifth call when Logan appeared on the stairs, hanging onto the rail like a pale ghost.

He looked awful, half-collapsing on a step.

Mom's hand went to her throat. "Logan?"

I felt as if I was going to burst into tears.

Finally Logan spoke in a hoarse voice. "It was . . . it was twenty-two-twenty." His lips twisted into a sloppy smile, suggesting he was about ready to bawl himself.

After a few seconds of silence, Mom whispered, "What did you say?"

"TWENTY-TWO-TWENTY!" Logan bellowed.

I jumped up from the couch, raced up the steps, and threw myself on my brother. P.S. crawled up to join us, while Mom tried to dial the phone with shaking fingers.

"Bill, it was twenty-two-twenty. Yes! No, I'm not kidding! It was just as great as I said it would be! It was just the best!"

When she hung up, Logan hauled himself off the step, tottered down into the living room on shaky legs, and headed for the phone.

"Calling your friends to let them know?" Mom beamed.

Logan picked up the phone and held it a few seconds. "Actually," he said finally, "I'm calling Mary Pat."

Mom's smile froze on her lips. So did mine. All this success, and he was getting back with Mary Pat?

He punched in numbers. "Hello? Hi, it's Logan. I just . . . no, wait . . . don't go there. I just wanted to tell you that I did really well on the test. I wanted to, um, thank you. I really appreciate all you did for me. Please don't cry, Mary Pat." He paced with the receiver, listening. "We can't do that. It just wouldn't work. I'm sorry. But we're still friends, okay?"

Finally he put the phone back on the hook. "Whew!"

Mom and I exchanged stunned looks. Logan was actually smiling as he headed for the kitchen.

He got out two frying pans and made mounds of scrambled eggs smothered in cheese and a skillet of fried potatoes and onions. He toasted bread, set out jam, butter, and ketchup, and made hot chocolate. "I'm still working on reducing saturated fat," he said through a full mouth. "But today, I celebrate!"

The next week we won our final game, giving a lot of play to the reserves. If our opponents' coaches, hidden in the stands and scribbling notes, had hoped to gain any clues, they were surely disappointed. We had won our division, and we were going to the playoffs.

But it was not going to be an easy ride. It became apparent, as we took on top-notch teams in frigid weather, that something was going wrong under the surface. We were playing good ball, but we weren't playing our best ball. We weren't playing the kind of ball that had beaten the Countryside Wildcats, Sugar Creek, and Hudson High. We didn't dominate the way we had most of the season.

Instead we held our opponents to low scoring games,

with our defense staying strong and creating turnovers, while Tony and Melvin fought for every yard and Brady kicked game-winning field goals.

With every win, the crowds swelled and became more boisterous, teachers slacked off on assigning homework, and Max once again got his picture in the local paper, even as the drunk yelled his abuse and presented his backside to the refs for what he deemed bad calls.

The tension between Cam and me was thicker than ever. We no longer spoke or even looked at each other. Our old chemistry on the field that had existed despite our first coolness was gone. He missed my patterns, misread my timing, and overthrew the ball. I missed my spots and dropped a few passes I should have nailed. The simple truth was that he didn't want to throw to me and I didn't want to receive from him.

It was a terrible situation, especially since next Saturday night, December 3, we would be at Canton's Fawcett Stadium, next door to the Pro Football Hall of Fame. We'd be playing the Cleveland Buckeyes for the High School Division II Ohio State Football Championship.

34

We were alone now. Each of us looked as scared as the next. Gone was that smug, invincible feeling of championship destiny.

Hearing discordant notes far in the distance, I grinned faintly. Our band had taken the field. I wondered if Logan would find his way tonight; I thought he might. He was more confident now and had sent off applications to half a dozen colleges, including Xavier and State.

Coach Miller laid down his chalk and stepped away from the board where he'd been outlining a couple of newer plays. Coaches Stanley and Brewster stood against the wall, clipboards under their arms, looking almost as nervous as the team.

In minutes we would leave the locker room and head onto the Astroturf field with its player-friendly rubber base. The stadium had a seating capacity of over twenty-two thousand, with a real graphics display board and a press box. The game would start at seven P.M. and be broadcast statewide. College scouts and coaches would be watching from all over, both in the stadium and on TV.

With trembling hands, I reached down to tuck my

jersey tighter into my pants. The locker room was chilly. I hated to leave it, but couldn't wait to leave it either. My dreams were out on the field. So were my fears.

"Fawcett Stadium may look big, guys," Coach said. Every eye was locked on his strong Iron Jaw face. "But really it's just another playing field. And when you go out there, you take everything that pertains to the game. And you leave everything else"—he pointed to the floor—"right here." His eyes traveled the room, going from face to face. "If you're feeling subpar, you leave that here. If you have an ego or attitude, it stays behind. If you're having a fight with your girl—leave it here. Lockdown for the next year of your life—leave it right here. Just got your first speeding ticket— it doesn't see the field.

"What you take with you when you leave that door is what is best in you. What is strongest, toughest, and most courageous. You take what made you want to play the game to begin with. You take your speed, your daring. You take your determination. Most of all, you take your confidence in yourself and in each other. Look around you, men. This is your team."

In the dead silence, players' eyes traveling around the room, I remembered walking up the hill into the park between Tony and Brian, the offensive line moving ahead of us, taking the heat, as always. I nodded to the offensive guards and tackles, to our runners and tight ends, to the defense and the special teams. But it was hard to look at certain faces and to remember they had been on the other team that day.

Cam was up front, closest to the chalkboard. He never

lifted his head or nodded. In fact, he hadn't said a word since he'd dressed for the game.

"Something else that stays here," Coach said, "is any bad blood between two players. It has no place on the field. Out there, we are one. There may be disagreements in the other world, but there is no animosity in our ranks. We play as a unit. Because no one player in this room can take on that team out there alone. Not Ed Bent, even though he's got a lot of colleges looking to recruit him next year. Not Cam, not Joey. Not Melvin Barr, no matter how tough the Ohio State college scout told me he looked during our last game."

Melvin's head jerked up. "He did?"

Coach's lips twitched. "He mentioned it. He thinks a lot of good things about a lot of individual players in this room. But if we don't play as a unit, we cannot beat Cleveland High School. We lost two games this season. Cleveland"—he held up a circle between index finger and thumb—"lost none. Not one game. But if every man on our team plays his best, and if the team plays as a unit, then I know we can finally beat this unbeatable team."

He looked at us, smiling slightly. "What do you say?"

From all over the room it came thundering: "YEAAAAH!"

Coach nodded. "Let's go, men."

Then there was only the sound of cleats on concrete as we followed him from the locker room into the lights of Fawcett Stadium.

35

We ran through the cheerleaders' tunnel and straight into pandemonium.

The Bulldogs' crowd was on its feet yelling its heart out. Somewhere up in that crowd of waving pompoms and cardboard signs, Mom, Dad, P.S., and all three of my grandparents were sitting with Sam and her mom. Tony's mom was up there, too, with his youngest sisters, along with Alice. Logan, Perry, and Tony's oldest sister were with the pounding drums of the band. Mrs. Cunningham was in the stands. Even Kelsey and Ted had both assured me they would be there in support. I saw Max in one of the guy cheerleader's arms, struggling to get to me as I ran past him onto the most beautiful field I had ever seen in my life.

I took one look at Cam, trotting along beside me. His face could have been carved out of a glacier. I hated him even now, despite what the coach had told us about not bringing any baggage onto the field. But somehow I had to make it right with him. Just for tonight. Tonight we needed all our guns.

If Cam had nodded at me, or smiled in my general direction, or even just met my eyes once, it would have helped heal the rift between us. But the remote look on his face froze me completely.

We were in trouble from the first play. On the opening kickoff, the Buckeyes' return man broke through our special team coverage and returned the ball sixty-five yards to our twenty-yard line. They ran the ball hard at us and in three beautifully executed plays had a 7-0 lead.

Covering my face with a towel, I tried to shake off the feeling of doom that had settled inside me.

The pumped-up Buckeyes kicked off. Our blocking was sloppy and Tony was smothered after only a ten-yard return. I wondered if the rest of the team had the same butterflies I did because after a bad snap from George at center, the Buckeyes recovered Cam's fumble.

Heads down, faces stained red, we ran to the sidelines and were forced to watch the Buckeyes' all-star quarterback throw a twenty-six yard post to their flanker for a second touchdown.

Only two minutes into the game, and we were already digging a deep hole for ourselves.

The drunk was there. I heard him yelling above the rest with his usual foul language. Any minute now, security would be closing in on him. Hopefully they'd get to him before he started throwing things onto the field again.

On the sidelines Coach Miller went from player to player, trying to settle us down. "Stay cool. Keep calm. Play your game. Don't try to get it back all at once. One play at a time. That's how we'll get back into this game."

Slowly we began to find our rhythm. Tony made good yardage, and our tight ends made several catches for first downs. But Cam's two passes to me both went incomplete. After that Coach didn't call my number again. It was all too obvious that he had lost confidence in the combination of McKey and Eastland. Instead he called for short passes to the ends and relied on our running game.

It was mainly Cam, Brian, and Tony that were featured on the big graphics screen at the top of the stadium that ran replays and closed in tight on the players.

I wanted another shot, but it didn't come. Trying to put away my disappointment, I concentrated on getting in every possible block, more than one of them helping to give us a first down. It was better than sitting on the bench, even if my ribs were aching. Finally we got close enough to the goal line for Melvin to muscle in our first TD. On our next possession, Brady kicked a field goal.

By halftime, we were down 20-10.

Back in the locker room, Coach reminded us we had to be ready for the fake punt we had practiced earlier in the week. Hopefully we wouldn't need it, but he went over it again just in case and then handed his clipboard to Coach Stanley, leaving him to finish the team notes. "Cam, Joey. I want to see you. Over there." He pointed to a row of lockers.

Cam and I followed him without looking at each other.

Coach put his back against a locker, facing us. "Listen to me," he said. "The Buckeyes didn't get this far by being a dumb team. They see that we aren't throwing the ball downfield. That means they don't have to worry about the long pass at all, giving them the luxury to key in on our runners. You can change all that in one play."

He turned to Cam. "How can you pass, if you won't

look at your receiver?" He shifted his gaze to me. "Eastland, how can you catch if you won't look at your quarterback?"

When neither of us answered him, Coach took each of us by the shoulder and turned us to face one another. He said, "Look each other in the eye, because for this next half, that's all you've got. Each other. You got it? We're gonna start going deep, guys."

Cam still said nothing, but he looked me in the eye. Coach's orders. Feeling hollow inside, I gazed back at him.

Coach nodded. "It's a start. I'll see you both on the field. Good luck." He turned and left us standing there, still staring at each other.

My lips moved trying to say something. I think it was "good luck." But Cam turned without a word and followed the Coach out of the locker room and onto the field. Most of the team trailed behind them. I slammed my helmet into a locker, the metallic twang echoing through the almost empty room. Then after a long moment, I picked it up and walked toward the door.

Tony had waited for me. Together we filed out after the rest.

We started down the middle of the bleachers and headed for the lights. It was a world I'd grown to love. The field, the other players, and the crowd. The announcer's voice up in the booth. The refs and the lit scoreboard. The sound of cleats on concrete, then the feel of them digging into the ground as we ran onto the field.

Somehow the big stadium became smaller, blending into my memories of our own home field. I could almost smell the "Bull" dogs from the snack bar. Standing on dry Astroturf on a crisp, cold night, I could smell the rain-soaked earth from the last game we'd played on our home field. I remembered playing in snow for the first time. I loved it. All of it.

"Hey, hotshot," a thick voice slurred.

I turned and saw the drunk hanging on the fence, his face up against the chain-link. He was looking right at me with total hatred on his face.

Shocked, I stared back at him, hardly aware that Tony had run past me, heading to the bench in preparation for the kickoff return.

"Yeah, I'm talking to you," the drunk said again. "The little wart that thought he could be a football player."

I felt my face heat up, then I straightened and looked into his watery eyes. His mouth was so weak and lopsided it seemed to be melting at the edges. Liquid seeped from his nose. He wore expensive clothes, all except for his Bulldog sweatshirt. His long coat was made of suede, his boots looked like a pair I had seen that cost two hundred dollars, and he wore an exotic fur hat. But there was a smear of mustard on his coat and a stain spreading across his sweatshirt. Under the fur hat, his glare was so intense I could feel myself swallowing.

"You're out of your class here, kid," he wheezed. "No use to pretend different. I know all about you, even drove by to look at your father's two-bit store. I could buy and sell him a thousand times over. I hear you even have a little black boy as your best friend. How does it feel to be white trash?"

Though I didn't say a word, he saw my fury. "Why don't you come through that door if you're so mad?" He pointed at the chain-link exit. "Come on, I dare you." His hands were fists, his smile eager.

Hold it, Joey. You've been playing ball long enough to know a trick play when you see one. It was the GR.

Still speechless, I stood my ground, inches from the leering face. In a single explosive *pff!* he spat at me through the fence.

I drew a shaky breath and stepped backward, mind reeling as I dried my face with my sleeve and tried to figure what this was all about. It didn't make sense.

"Who are you?" I muttered. "Why do you hate me so much?"

Before he could answer, a voice spoke behind me.

"A lot of reasons," it said flatly. "You aren't rich, you don't hang out with the right crowd, and you've gotten more good press than his son."

It was a voice I recognized. I turned slowly to face Cam. His face was flushed deep red. He met my gaze squarely and did not turn away.

"Another reason he probably doesn't like you much," Cam went on in the same wooden voice, "is because you've taken Matt's position on the team. He takes that personally. You see, he and Matt's dad used to get drunk together at the games."

He looked at the drunk with sick eyes. "It's not as much fun being a solitary drunk, is it? And it must be a hell of a lot harder to throw trash barrels over the fence by yourself." He turned back to me. "I'm sorry, Joey."

I looked back at the drunk and then at Cam, startled and confused. "I don't get it, Cam."

Cam swallowed several times, then slowly opened his mouth. "He's my dad," he whispered.

There was a rush of foul words, directed at Cam this time, but neither of us even looked toward the fence. Standing there in Fawcett Stadium, looking at the shame in Cam's eyes, my anger died. I wanted to say something, to help him in some way. But there was nothing I could do, nothing I could say. I thought of all the rotten things he'd done, things I'd thought I could never forgive.

I mumbled something under my breath, and Cam frowned, not hearing.

"What?"

"Nothing." What I'd muttered was "the power of understanding." All that time with Mrs. C. and until that moment, standing there looking at Cam, I'd never really gotten it.

The horn blew, signaling the second half. Both special teams began filing onto the field.

"Cam?"

"Yeah?"

I drew a deep breath and stuck out my hand. "Why don't we go kick some butt?"

He took my hand and we shook. "Sure, Receiver," he said. "Let's do it. Let's win this thing."

From what seemed very far away, the drunk once again began to yell. But neither of us looked back. Together, Cam and I jogged toward the rest of our team.

*   *   *

Our defense held the Buckeyes' first possession and they had to punt. We started our own drive at our twenty-five with a pass to Brian. But the Buckeyes were ready and took him down for no gain.

Then the Coach finally called my number again. It was the play our opponents had feared most all season, the long pass. Cam fired a rocket thirty yards downfield and hit me in stride, right between the numbers. It felt great. I tacked on another fifteen yards and we were deep in enemy territory.

And now that the Buckeyes feared our passing game, their defense loosened up. A seven-yard burst by Tony was followed by a four-yarder up the gut by Melvin for another first down.

This was the momentum Coach had been looking for. But on the next play, a screen pass to Tony ended in disaster. He caught the ball, avoided a tackle, and veered toward the sideline, only to take a full speed hit from the Buckeyes' all-state linebacker, Dante Morgan. He jerked Tony's arm hard; Tony went down. The ball flew into the arms of their cornerback, who had nothing but open field ahead of him and ran for a spectacular eighty-five yard touchdown.

Tony, who almost never fumbled, slammed his helmet against the bench and buried his head in his hands.

The coach came over. "Hold your head up, son; happens to the best. We need you out there, can't win without you."

Tony shuddered. Then he nodded, raised his head, and rubbed his sleeve over his eyes. He clenched his teeth and made himself watch the kicker put the ball through the uprights, making it 27-10. Then he was off the bench and back in action.

On the sidelines, our offense huddled up.

"We're in a deep hole," Coach Miller said, "but we're not dead yet. I believe in you. Win, lose, or draw, we're gonna give 'em all we've got. No reason to hold anything back."

The Buckeyes kicked off. Reversing his field, Tony started right and cut back to the left, broke a tackle, and ran the ball back to midfield. Coach wasted no time in calling my number. On a post pattern, Cam put a little extra zip on his spiral and I hauled it in on the twenty-yard line. The next play, Cam rolled right and found me in the corner of the end zone. I brought it in with two hands and no celebrating beyond a private little "Yeah!"

Touchdown. 27-16 now.

Coach called for a two-point conversion, and on a quarterback draw, Cam pounded his way across the goal line to make it 27-18.

The rest of the third quarter, and halfway into the fourth, both teams played their best defense, but the Buckeyes added a field goal. At 30-18, it was getting to be crunch time.

On a third and six from midfield, the Buckeyes blitzed, and Cam couldn't pick up his outlet receiver. Five minutes to go and fourth down. Out came our punt team. Our offense left the field, except for Tony. He stayed where he was, joining the special team that had some of our tallest players. Tony had never looked so small.

On the sidelines, Cam leaned over to me and said quietly, "This is it."

We stood together and watched what we knew was

coming, though some of the guys buried their heads in their hands or in their towels. Every Bulldog knew it could be our last offensive play of the season.

All I could see was Tony. If anything goes wrong, don't let it be his fault, I thought. I was glad it was Brady, our kicker and punter, out there. A cooler head didn't exist on the field.

The ref's whistle blared.

Brady took the snap and started to punt.

Tony was off and running. In a flash, Brady lofted a soft spiral into the flat to him. Tony put it away and stepped out of bounds.

First down!

Cam and about five players grabbed me.

The whole stadium went crazy, our side cheering and the other side shocked into silence. We saw it all happen again on the graphics scoreboard. It looked even better the second time.

We had practiced that fake punt all week. "Just in case," the coach had said. "Just in case" had just paid off.

Our offense ran back onto the field, juiced up and ready to move the ball. You could feel our confidence growing as we worked our way downfield. Eight-yard pass to Mr. Freeze. Five-yard run from Melvin. We were in the zone.

A bullet came at me over the middle. I took off running and never looked back, flying past the ref who had both arms straight up in the air.

Touchdown! The extra point was good. With just under four minutes to go, the scoreboard showed 30-25.

Frozen with tension, I watched the Coach gather the

defense close. The kickoff had taken the Buckeyes to their twenty-five yard line.

"We're putting the show in your hands now, men," he said without a trace of the panic that crawled in my own belly. "If the Buckeyes get even one first down, this game is history. They get *nothing* from you. You hear me? Nothing!"

Ricardo Gonzalez met his gaze squarely, his face that strange blend of calm and fury found on the faces of linebackers called on to do the impossible. "Trust me, Coach. Not a single *yard*."

On all sides of him, heads nodded. Their body language was easy to read as they strode forward, following their defensive leader onto the field. It was crunch time and the best defense in the league was not about to take any prisoners.

On the Buckeyes' first play, I felt like I was watching a swarm of hornets. It was the most ferocious defensive rush I'd ever seen. Their runner was creamed for a three-yard loss, with the clock running.

Second down. They ran into a brick wall of red jerseys for another loss, with more time clicking away.

"One more time," Cam muttered. "Just get us the ball."

Third and fifteen, the Buckeyes tried a sweep, and five Bulldogs mauled the runner and gang-tackled him for another loss. Gonzalez had delivered on his promise: Not a single yard!

If there had been a dome, it would have blown off the stadium. The fired-up Bulldog fans rose as one to give Gonzalez and his posse a roaring standing ovation. They were still stamping and screaming as the punt return team came on the field. *"GO BULLDOGS!!!"*

We got the ball at our forty-yard line with a minute ten to go. We all put our hands together in the center of our huddle. "We can do this," Cam said. "Let's show 'em what we're made of, guys."

A seven-yarder to Mr. Freeze was followed by a quick hustle to the line, and an audible for a six-yarder to Tony in the flat.

The first down let us huddle up. Cam nodded my way. "Ready? Trips right, slot out. On two."

In serious hurry-up mode, he fired a twenty-three yarder to me over the middle. With the coaches waving furiously, we scrambled back into formation. Cam's call was an audible: "Blue, single-out, *hut-hut!*"

The play was an eight-yarder to Brian. Coach used a time-out, leaving us with one more. We had nineteen seconds, with the ball on their thirty-two yard line. My number was called again. "Twins right. Double post on three."

The play lined Wayne and me up on the right. He ran an outside route and I flew toward the goal line on the inside. Cam fired a perfect spiral to me. It was a catch, and two tacklers brought me down at the eleven-yard line.

Coach yelled for our last time-out. With five seconds left to play, Cam went to the sidelines, leaving us to wait silently until he came back to the huddle with the play.

"Shotgun, spread left, Z 23 motion out, halfback hot on two." His face looked about twenty years older, but he managed a grin. "Coach said to tell everybody to breathe."

The play was designed for me to make the game-winning catch with Brian as backup receiver. For a second I saw myself crossing the goal line with the ball in my hands.

"Cam," I said just before we broke the huddle, "they'll be keying on me with double, maybe even triple, coverage. They'll have somebody on Brian, too. If we're both covered, Tony should be open. Get the ball to him. I'll take out Morgan."

Cam and Tony both looked at me. Dante Morgan was the biggest guy on the field and the toughest.

Tony's face told me he hadn't forgotten Morgan ripping the ball out of his hands earlier, but he nodded, meeting my eyes squarely. "I'll be ready."

Cam said, "Let's do it, guys."

The snap came to Cam and he rolled right. I waved my hands as though I expected the pass. Sure enough the Buckeyes were double covering me, and a linebacker was in hot pursuit of Brian. Without missing a beat, Cam found Tony in the right flat and fired him a bullet. This was my cue to race back to the middle and take out Dante Morgan. By now the cornerback who had been covering me was on top of Tony, but Tony made a heck of a juke around him on the five-yard line. Now there was only Morgan coming from the middle between Tony and the goal line.

I dug for every ounce of speed that I had in me and headed for Morgan on a direct collision course. With Tony streaking toward the end zone, Morgan was about two feet away from him and coming on hard. I yelled and threw myself into a gear I didn't know I had. A second before Morgan could take Tony down I blindsided him with the hardest block I had ever thrown.

The collision took us both down. I never saw Tony dive over the goal line. It was the roar from the Bulldogs' cheering section that told me that he had just made the game-winning touchdown.

Dante Morgan looked at me, and we lay there together with tears in our eyes. Neither of us was ashamed to cry. But he was a champion. He got up, held out a hand, and pulled me to my feet.

"Thanks, man," I told him. "Great game."

"You too," he said gruffly.

I looked toward the goal line and saw Tony there with the ball held high over his head and the Bulldogs swarming him. The guys lifted him on their shoulders, and suddenly it all became real. We were the new Division II Ohio State Champions.

Somebody spun me around. It was Coach Miller.

"Did I tell you a block can win a game?" He slapped me on the helmet and then grabbed me in a bear hug. "One of these days, when you're one of the great receivers, Eastland, never forget that the guy who made the block earned himself part of that touchdown." He smiled. "I never forgot the linemen who blocked for me. Go enjoy it, boy. You're a champion now."

"Thanks, Coach."

I went running and got a hand on Tony, walking along behind Cam who had been the first to lift him up. I wanted to be part of the crew that carried my friend around the field of Fawcett Stadium.

36

Just before winter break, "The Power of Understanding" did a presentation before the student body. I sat in the auditorium with my fellow students and watched our animated film. We all sat mesmerized as Stump, the jolly tree spirit, opened his trunk and welcomed us to his joyful world—a place where people of every nationality, color, size, and shape cavorted to exuberant music played by the one un-animated girl in the entire film. It was Kelsey Magnum, her violin under her chin, playing her heart out, looking happier than I had ever imagined she could. She was barefoot and draped in ancient Grecian-style attire, with flowers in her blond hair and forest creatures dancing around her. The audience burst into applause at the end when Stump, Kelsey, and the animated characters all took their bows.

Mrs. Cunningham finally waved the auditorium to silence. "We have much more in the works for our international presentation, but for now," she said, smiling, "we will hear just one essay."

She motioned to Sam, sitting next to me in the first row, and Sam got up and walked to the podium.

The auditorium was silent. How in the world could Sam follow what we had just seen? But Samantha flashed a dazzling smile, cleared her throat, and said playfully, "My essay is entitled *How Can I Like You When You Refuse to Belch at My Dinner Table?*"

A roar of laughter filled the auditorium. Then everyone bent forward, listening to her every word. Who would have thought my girl could get as much applause as Stump himself?

The night of the Wacky Winter Dance, it wasn't the big silver ball that sent light dancing across the floor that made me dizzy.

It was Sam. She was wearing a shimmering blue dress that was cut to show she had one of the best figures in the room. Her skin glowed and her lips shone. Her eyes were big blue-green headlights. Half the guys in the room, including Brady and Cam, were staring at her. But she mostly looked at me.

"I think the dancing has gone really well," she said, reminding me of the nights we'd spent practicing in her basement. "We could give it a rest though."

I found myself a little disappointed. They were playing a slow dance. There was something about being this close to Sam that felt really good.

"You want to sit down?" I made a move toward our table.

"No, I just meant we could do a little less . . . dancing." She smiled and nodded toward Tony and Alice. Alice had her arms draped over Tony's shoulders. His arms were around her waist, and their cheeks were together. They were swaying more than dancing, though.

Tony caught my eye, grinned and winked.

I blushed, but before I knew what she was doing, Sam stepped closer and put her arms over my shoulders. I was so surprised I stumbled. Only now I wasn't worried about who saw me trip. I'd dropped enough passes to know that nobody plays a perfect game.

Holding Sam close, I looked around the big room. If there ever had been a loop, you wouldn't know it tonight. Either I had imagined it to begin with, or its boundaries weren't as rigid as I'd once thought. Either way, I just didn't care anymore. On all sides of us, people smiled and spoke to Sam and me. I had come a long way—and not just in football.

I wasn't on the outside anymore.

Sometimes you get in the zone just by knowing you're in it, the GR said. *And the opposite is also true.*

Matt hadn't come to the dance. Cam had broken up with Nancy Frazier a week ago and had shown up alone. He spent most of his time standing against the wall, talking to guys on the team, especially his offensive line. They were keyed on him tightly, as if discovering a quarterback whose buns might be worth saving after all come next season. Perry had shown me a personal apology letter that Cam had written him. Cam wasn't perfect; who was? But I knew he was trying to improve.

A thin high voice was raised over the music. I danced Sam closer to the punchbowl, where Perry was holding court, gesturing to a group around him, no doubt telling them more about the helicopter, which he was patenting himself, with money from his father.

"I'm glad Logan got a date," Sam murmured as we danced closer to the silver ball, the floor glittering under our feet.

"Yeah, me too."

Dead center under the ball, my brother was dancing with a girl from the band named Kaeleigh. She was about his size, had curly red hair, and was very cute. At first glance it was hard to see which one of them was leading.

On the other side of the room, I noticed a sad-looking Mary Pat steering her date across the floor. For her sake, I hoped he was a good candidate to take over her uncle's veterinary practice. For his sake, I hoped he could equalize the power structure.

Ashley smiled wistfully at me as she came dancing by with Brady. I cleared my throat and looked the other way.

"She never gives up, does she?" Sam whispered in my ear. "Look over there!"

I gasped, unable to believe my eyes. There, waltzing in a corner and lost in a world of their own, were gorgeous Kelsey Magnum and plain, big-eared and pimpled Ted Wyatt, wrapped in each other's arms.

"Wow, I would never have figured that one."

"Really?" Sam pulled back to smile at me.

"Come on, don't tell me you knew!"

"Only from our second week on the project."

Dumbfounded, I shook my head at her knowing smile.

"I have to tell you something," she said.

"What?" I replied, inhaling her perfume.

She pulled her cheek away from mine and looked into my eyes with her usual serious expression. "I think you are the coolest, most good-looking, neatest guy that I ever met," she said.

Now she really had me blushing.

"You're kidding," I said, "because I was just thinking that you are the coolest girl that *I* ever met. You are also the nicest. And every guy in the room already knows you're the prettiest."

We smiled at each other and kept on dancing. It felt as good as winning the championship game.